THE
KENNEDY
CURSE

Also by Bill Olver

Clones, Fairies & Monsters in the Closet (editor, 2013)
APESHIT (editor, 2013)

THE
KENNEDY
CURSE

Edited by
BILL OLVER

Exter Press

Credits

Accidents Happen © 2013 Nick Andreychuk
The Kennedy Tour © 2013 R.H. Blackburn
Marilyn's Vows © 2013 Patricia Bruce
Fathers, Sons, Ghosts, Guns © 2013 Gary Cahill
Bobby's Close Shave © 2013 Harri B. Cradoc
Out of Frame © 2013 Jarrid Deaton
Holy Day © 2013 Liz Dolan
The Cost of Freedom © 2013 Milo James Fowler
How the Mighty Have Fallen © 2013 Raymond Gallucci
Non Compos Mentis © 2013 A.A. Garrison
No More War Redux © 2013 Walter Giersbach
Camelot, Mariner Year 1962 © 2013 John Grey
The Night Kennedy Got Shot © 2013 Atar Hadari
Canvassing the Vote, Cuckold, The Plutocrat © 2013 John Hayes
KC © 2013 L.L. Hill
Two Brothers Fighting, A Lonely Actress, A Patsy? © 2013 Jack Horne
The Cuban Exile Crisis © 2013 Tony Laplume
Mountain Of God © 2013 Tim Lieder
Last Will of Little Rosie © 2013 Paul Lorello
Debts of the Father © 2013 Zoe McAuley
A Bullet's All it Takes © 2013 Terrence McCauley
Camelot © 2013 James Penha
The Curse of Brian Boru © 2013 Terrie Leigh Relf
Rosemary's Lobotomy, Salute, Goin' to the Moon © 2013 James Frederick
William Rowe
The Winners © 2013 E.F. Schraeder
Body Dump © 2013 Mike Sharlow
Boiler Room Girl © 2013 R.J. Spears
Hannah's Darling © 2013 Anna Sykora
Ode to O's Clothes © 2013 Sarah Delap U

Cover illustration © 2013 Robert Hand and Phil Good

The Kennedy Curse

ISBN 978-0-9896812-0-9

Visit us online:
www.bigpulp.com
www.exterpress.com
Facebook (Facebook.com/bigpulp)
Twitter (twitter.com/BigPulp)

Distributed by Ingram Periodicals.

Ebook versions available from Amazon
and other online venues

Exter Press
BILL OLVER Editor/Publisher
BILL BOSLEGO Associate Editor (Editorial)
PHIL GOOD Associate Editor (Art Direction)

TABLE OF CONTENTS

Cover illustration by Robert Hand and Phil Good

THE CURSE OF BRIAN BORU

by Terrie Leigh Relf

Circa 1000, Killaloe, County Clare, Ireland

The Shannon was raging beneath the crescent moon's wan light. That, and an eerie wind had risen, threatening to dash the bridge joining the shores of Killaloe with Limerick to splinters. Meadhbh shivered behind a bern of moss-covered stones, wondering if she should just run the remaining distance, but her limbs were frozen in place.

But it was their king, Brian Boru, not the natural elements, that cast the cold inside her very bones, lying claim even to the marrow. Brian Boru and the uncanny light surrounding him like a midmorning spring rather than this wintry moonless night.

Meadhbh's older sister, Síle, had sent her on an errand to their mother's sister, Aoife, to get some herbs and whatnot to banish the winter chill consuming their parents. It was usually safe to walk the fairly short distance from her parents' house to her aunts', even in the dark, especially since most of the men had gone up to Beal Boruma. Conflict was once again brewing in the land, and yon Brian was at the heart of it, as usual.

Brian didn't resemble their king in the slightest as he stood awash in the unnatural light. From the look of him, Brian was unafraid. Was he really so brave as all that, or had he been visited before? Even the earth itself seemed to rumble beneath the weight of the light and what was assuredly a most horrendous purpose. Meadhbh shielded her eyes the best she could, willing to remain undiscovered.

No one needed to tell her no good would come from spying on their liege. It wasn't as if she had followed him here, but here she was nevertheless. And there *he* was, waiting beneath some otherworldly contraption—for contraption is what it surely was. As Brian held his arms aloft, he was hoisted—and without the aid of ropes—through an opening surrounded by pulsing crystals, until he disappeared from view like a shadow snared by midmorning sun.

The contraption reminded her of a cave she had crawled into once, where jagged teeth of transparent stone had gnawed at her arms and legs. She had heard voices in that cave, voices that had murmured to her in unknown tongues, and she had scrabbled out, but not before collecting fragments to show her aunt Aoife who knew about such things.

As the orb receded into the starless night, Meadhbh exhaled violently as if someone had slammed her on the back. While she caught her breath, Meadhbh's ears popped, followed by a crackling in her jaw and neck. Had she been so tense? Or was it the proximity to the orb that had affected her so?

She ran the rest of the way to Aoife's house, wondering what, if anything, she should say about it. "Just the truth, girl," her aunt would probably say, for truth was always the best course with her aunt. The woman could *see* things, *know* things that no one else knew.

As Meadhbh walked alongside the stone house toward the porch, she saw that her aunt was already out front, waiting. Then Meadhbh realized Aoife was staring at the same spot in the sky where the orb had disappeared with Brian.

"So you saw it, didn't you, child. And him as went with them…" She pursed her full lips, tucked a wisp of blue black hair into a woolen scarf. "Tsk, and you've been clambering about in the moss again! Inside with you for a bit of warm stew before you catch a chill."

Meadhbh nodded, gathering the edges of her cloak around her to step onto the porch and through the open door.

"Yon Brian Boru is up to no good with these goings-on, I'm afraid. Now, then, Meadhbh, dear," she said, closing and barring the wooden door, then fixing her with dark unfathomable eyes, "do tell me what it is you saw."

◊ ◊ ◊ ◊ ◊

Brian Boru didn't return to his castle that night, or the next day or night, either.

There were whisperings about Killaloe that he was meeting with neighboring clans or that the Vikings of Limerick wanted to have a word with him. A few even went so far as to say he was visiting the monastic island in search of guidance. The old ones just winked, jutting their chins toward a narrow path leading around the hill to a particular cottage where rumor had it, their liege kept one of several young mistresses.

When several days turned into a fortnight, Brian's clan started a search to no avail. They were beginning to think their leader had met with foul play or the Shannon had taken him into its icy embrace.

Meadhbh and her aunt, Aoife, however, kept what they had seen to themselves. Not even Síle, who had enough to worry about with their ailing parents, was privy to what Aoife and Meadhbh knew.

And they planned to keep it that way. For no good would come of sharing this knowledge.

When Brian reappeared at fortnight's end, he acted as if no time had passed at all, and was aghast and grumbling at all the fuss. "Can't a man have some peace and quiet to consider his own counsel?" he bellowed to the gathering throng.

As the crowd parted to let him pass, Aoife's almond eyes narrowed even further. There was something a bit off about yon Brian. A subtle change to his eyes, as if glimmering moss had taken root within the brown earth of his eyes. He walked a bit stiffly, too, as if he had slept out in the cold, and yet...there was an odd spring to his usual solid and deliberate steps, as if he had found new purpose.

As the weeks wore on, there were whisperings about the king's moods in the market place. A few household servants had been going on about the odd bouts of silence, more disturbing than his usual boisterous speech. "He sits at table not touching his meal, just staring into the fire," one said, while another offered, "He has some sort of amulet beneath his shirt that no one, not even the most clever of us, has been able to see up close."

Late winter became early spring and there were rumors of

a conflict brewing to the north. So, when the first few cows disappeared, there were a few shrugs and comments about thieves in the night or perhaps a forgotten barter between neighbors longing for passage to warmer climes. Since it is in their nature to wander about, most people thought that's what happened. They just wandered off and would wander home shortly. But when even more cows, a cherished bull, and several early calves disappeared, there was pandemonium. Were they and their families safe? How would they feed their families? Who would trade milk and cheese for dried roots and a bit of oil?

Then a swarm of flies led to a single cow…

Its mutilated corpse was discovered on the other side of the hill. While it had clearly once been a cow, the remaining tangled mass of limbs and gore took a moment to decipher. And if that wasn't strange enough, the very moisture seemed to have been absorbed from the surrounding earth as well. One of the men scratched his stubble, then drew a circle in the air. Everyone backed away.

There were other whisperings, too. "Someone's consorting with the devil—or worse—in Killaloe!" And so the village was locked up tight at night, down to the last cow and sheep in the barn. Guards stood vigil through the night and into the day for several weeks, and not a cow or sheep disappeared. Killaloe exhaled a collective sigh of relief.

But then the first girl disappeared…and then the next and the next. Girls not yet married, girls just before and after their first blood. Those who had seen the cow's remains shuddered beneath the warm spring sun.

Killaloe wanted to declare war—but on whom?

Or what?

Given the rights of men and kings, Brian had been known to stray from his wife's bed. An occasional rumor declared his prowess between the furs had resulted in more than a few dark-haired bairns. But other than a few girls robbed of their maidenhood, their angry fathers and grandfathers appeased by a purse or two of coin, a sack of grain, nothing worse had ever befallen them at Brian's hand.

Brian Boru may have been many things, but he wasn't a murderer of women and children.

Or so it was believed until the night Aoife once again witnessed the strange lights over the Shannon, and Brian disappeared again.

On the following day, Síle visited Aoife to pick up Meadhbh only to learn the girl had never arrived. In the way she knew things, Aoife claimed that yon Brian and his orb of light were to blame, and in her rage, she vowed Brian Boru, king or no, and all his descendants for all time would pay.

And so they have.

A Bullet's All it Takes

by Terrence McCauley

HOTEL ALSCACE ~ LORRAINE
NEW YORK CITY
1926

Archie Doyle put the back of his hand against the silver coffee pot and frowned.

"Goddamned thing's colder than an Eskimo's ass." He opened the lid and sniffed. "Still smells good, though. Hot or cold, good coffee's still good coffee." He looked over at Quinn. "Want some?"

"No thanks, boss," Quinn said. "Coffee this late keeps me up."

Doyle grabbed one of the two used cups on the dinner cart and began cleaning it out with a dirty dinner napkin. He smiled as he wiped the inside of the cup clean. "Napkin's got lipstick on it. The cup, too. Figure it must be Gloria's, so I might as well use that one, seein' as how her and me are on a familiar basis and all."

Quinn felt himself smiling, too. He didn't know who Gloria was, but only Doyle could break into a man's hotel room and think to offer coffee.

Quinn had seen his fair share of tough men in his day. Prohibition had produced a bumper crop of two-bit hoods and bullies looking to strong-arm their way to big money. Most of them were just wind and piss. Punks who didn't have heart or stamina or brains.

But Doyle was tough right down to his core and all the way around the track. He was Five Points born and bred. He never ran or backed down which was the only reason why he'd gotten as far as he had in the criminal underworld. And he did it with a sense of style that Quinn admired.

For example: another hood would've waited to grab their target while he walked down the street or cornered him while he was at dinner with his wife or girlfriend. But not Archie. He wanted to make a point and figured the best place to make it would be in the man's own hotel suite. Nice and private. Not to mention nice and personal.

Doyle poured himself a cup of cold coffee and sipped it. He swallowed it down and licked his lips; just like some snobs did when they tasted wine. He took another sip and said, "Not bad. Would be better hot, but beggars can't be choosers, given present circumstances and all."

Quinn watched Doyle sit back and take in the suite like a kid at the zoo for the first time. Even with only one lamp on, it was easy to see it was a real nice set up. Silver wall paper. Nice moulding on the walls. Expensive looking furniture and even a fireplace, too.

"Seems like our pal Joey is doing pretty good for himself. Think I'll ever be able to swing classy digs like this, kid?"

Doyle had always told Quinn to speak his mind, especially when asked, so that's what he did. "After tonight, boss, I think you'll be able to afford damned near anything you want."

Doyle looked down into his cup. "Making money is one thing, kid. Keeping it takes a hell of a lot of work. A lot of guys have found themselves on top of the heap one day only to find the heap on top of them the next. "

"You're not most guys, boss." Quinn nodded over to the bedroom door. "Want me to go in there and wake him up so we can get this over with?"

Doyle shook his head. "The weasel will hear us soon enough, if he hasn't already. And when he does come out, you just sit there and keep an eye on things. Joe's never been the type who liked gettin' his hands dirty, but you never know how a guy'll react when…"

Both Doyle and Quinn looked at the bedroom door when they heard the handle turn. The door opened inward and a tall, thin man paddled out into the living room wearing blue pajamas and matching slippers. The few hairs that had been raked across the top of his head were sticking up and his eyes were heavy from sleep. He tied the belt around his silk bathrobe, which was also blue.

"Who's there?" The man squinted as he fished his spectacles out of the robe's breast pocket. On that pocket was a monogram with three elaborately styled initials: JPK.

Joseph P. Kennedy.

"Evenin', Joey. Or should I say Good Mornin'." Doyle pulled out his pocket watch, looked at it. "Yep, it's goin' on one, so that makes it officially mornin'."

Kennedy's sleepiness quickly turned to indignation as he put on his spectacles and finally got a good look at his visitors. If he'd been looking at a couple of unicorns grazing on his leftovers, Quinn doubted he could've looked more surprised. "Archie Doyle? Is that you?"

Doyle smiled and threw open his hands. "The one and only. How've you been keepin' yourself, Joey? Long time, no hear."

"What in God's name are you doing here?" The more he thought about it, the angrier Kennedy seemed to get. "Are you drunk?"

He toasted Kennedy with the coffee cup. "Hard to get drunk on cold coffee. Even for me."

"What the hell are you doing in my room? And how did you get in here in the first place?" He spotted Quinn on the couch and squinted at him. Quinn looked right back. "And who's that thug you brought with you?"

Doyle sipped his cold coffee. "I'm afraid I've gotta correct you on two counts, Joey. First, this is technically a suite, not a room. Second, Quinn here ain't a thug. He's what you might call my associate. And he's also pretty handy when it comes to opening hotel room locks."

"I don't care if he's the king of England," Kennedy said, "he's got as much reason for being here as you do. I'll not tolerate this nonsense any further. I want the both of you to get the hell out of here before I call the police."

"We're not goin' anywhere and you're not callin' anyone." Doyle held up the napkin stained with lipstick.

Quinn noticed that Kennedy looked shaken for a second, but only for a second.

Doyle kept talking. "New York cops ain't like Boston cops. They come in here, they're liable to take a look around. See who else is here." He smiled as he set the napkin back down. "You wouldn't want a scandal, now would you, Joey? What would Rose think?"

Quinn watched the pale man turn red as he quietly closed the bedroom door behind him. "I think you're forgetting yourself, Mr. Doyle. And I think you've forgotten who it is you're talking to."

"No, I know exactly who I'm talking to, my friend. And a few hours ago, I wouldn't have talked to you this way. Hell, I didn't have be any reason to be up here in the first place. But lots of things can happen when the sun goes down in this town." He toasted him with his cup. "And, brother, a lot of things have happened this very night."

Kennedy closed his eyes and let out a long, slow breath. When he opened them, he was no longer just some poor sap who'd been woken up in the middle of the night. Now he was Joseph P. Kennedy, Boston power broker and all that it implied. Pajamas or no. "I'm not the least bit interested in anything a two-bit thug like you might have to say, Doyle. So you might as well just crawl back to the gutter from which you came and let me get back to sleep."

Doyle winked over at Quinn. "Did you get a load of that? That Boston bray? Those steely eyes? He can sure pour it on when he wants to, can't he?" Then he looked back at Kennedy. "That lace-curtain Irish routine might go over with the poor Micks up in Boston, boyo, but it don't cut shit with me. I don't give a damn how much money you've got or what schools you went to. You're still just another immigrant kid one generation off the boat, just like me."

Quinn watched Kennedy slide his hands into the pockets of his silk bathrobe. He looked for a bulge that might be a gun, but all he saw was the outline of Kennedy's slender hands. "You and I are nothing alike. I've made something of myself and have the money and connections to prove it. You're a two-bit hoodlum. A convicted felon. A mindless gutter snipe. The only thing we have in common is heritage and even that link is doubtful."

Doyle grinned through the insult. "Don't sell yourself short, Joey. We've got a lot more in common than just the old sod, you and me. We're both rum runners, after all, which makes us practically family."

"The importation of alcohol is illegal, Mr. Doyle, as you know perfectly well. You should. It's the only reason why you have two nickels to rub together. God knows you're not fit to do anything else."

Doyle waived him off. "Nah. I always found a way to make a buck even before Volstead. But you're a rum runner alright. Your ships bring your booze down from Nova Scotia every couple of days; regular as clock work, just like the post office. True, you're not man enough to be on the decks of your own ships, but you're a goddamned rum runner, alright. No better or worse than me."

The muscles in Kennedy's jaw flexed. "I'd appreciate it if you'd refrain from blasphemy in my presence."

Doyle wasn't smiling any more. "And I'd appreciate it if you'd quit trying to rip me off in my own backyard."

"And just what the hell is that supposed to mean?"

"It means that I know why you're down here in the first place. You just cut a deal with Masseria and his pals to screw me out of the bootleg business. And I'm not happy about it, either."

Quinn watched Kennedy to see if he reacted one way or the other, but he didn't. He just stood there with his hands in the pockets of his silk bathrobe and looked down at Doyle with narrow, nasty eyes behind his round spectacles. He looked more like a banker than a bootlegger and played the part well. "I'm afraid I haven't the slightest idea what you're talking about."

"Don't bother denying it," Doyle said. "I know you met them at a spaghetti joint down on the Lower East Side. And I know they told you they were pushin' me out. I know all of this because one of Masseria's boys told me."

This time, Quinn noticed Kennedy blinked quickly a few times before saying: "Assuming such a conversation with this Masseria fellow took place—and I'm certainly not admitting any such conversation happened—why in the world would they tell you something like that?"

Doyle motioned for Quinn to speak, so he did. "Because I caught Benny Siegel and beat it out of him. He's pretty tough for a pretty boy, but not tough enough."

"Benny Siegel?" Kennedy forced a laugh. "Sounds like a vaudeville comedian."

"Don't know how funny he is but he sings pretty good." Doyle finished his coffee and poured himself another cup. "Quinn's what your Italian buddies might call a *maestro* when it comes to giving singing lessons. A regular fuckin' Caruso."

Kennedy may have bristled from the vulgarity. Or it may have been because Doyle had him dead to rights.

Doyle went on. "I'm not particularly sore at you for lookin' for a better deal. Hell, we're all in this to make a buck anyway, so loyalty don't apply. I just wanted you to realize that this is what happens when you deal with people you don't fully understand."

Kennedy just kept looking at him. "I understand more than you know."

"Nah. You just think you do. Masseria and his boys talk a good game, but they've never left the street. Can they move your hooch for you? Sure. Will they pay more for it than me, probably. But they don't have my overhead, see? And overhead is what makes our dirty world keep turnin'. Because New York is still a Tammany town and I run Tammany. I handle the payoffs that keep the cops at bay. I run the politicians who pass the laws both down here and up in Albany. Not to mention all the speakeasies, gambling dens and other establishments I run. The guineas have the whorehouses and the heroin, so they've got the cash to pay you more. But they're pimps at heart and pimps don't make for good bosses in the long run. There's only one man you need to deal with, Joey. And that man is me."

Kennedy smiled a thin smile. "For the moment."

"For as long as I want it and I still want it. Sure, Masseria and his boys'll kick me out one day, but not until I'm good and ready to go. I've still got more men than they do and I still control everyone worth controlling in this town. The guineas will spill a lot of their own blood figurin' out whose gonna be the King Dago before it's all over and that's a headache you don't need. This is New York, not Chicago. And the cops here won't tolerate the same nonsense Capone's been pullin' out there. You want a better price, we can talk. But what I lack in dough, I make up for with influence and calm."

Kennedy didn't say anything for a bit. But Quinn could see he'd heard everything Doyle had told him and he was turning all of it over in his mind. Cold and calculating like the banker he was. "My product will get through somehow whether it's through you or them or someone else. What do I care if you and the Italians gut each other? I'll make money no matter what."

"You've got a point." Doyle poured himself some more cold coffee. "But there's the matter of the agreement you and me had about me bein' your exclusive customer in New York. An agreement you violated when you spoke to Masseria. I didn't get this far by lettin' agreements get ignored."

Kennedy pulled his hands out of his bathrobe and held them at his sides. Quinn checked to make sure they were empty and they were. When he spoke, there was more indignation than fear in his voice. "You're not actually dumb enough to be threatening me right now, are you?"

"Me? No." Doyle nodded at Quinn, who pulled his .45 from beneath his coat and aimed it at Kennedy's chest. "But he is."

Kennedy backed against the door. "Damn you, Doyle. You know who I am. Who I'm connected to?"

"Sure I do," Doyle said. "You were seen by a whole restaurant full of people tonight talking to a known underworld figure and his friends. Right about now, those same punks are gettin' shit-faced on cheap wine and runnin' their mouths to any whore within earshot on how they just cut a deal with Joseph P. Kennedy, himself. So, if you wind up found dead from a gunshot wound to the belly—and believe me, Joe, it will be to the belly—the cops will assume one of them must've done it. I'll make sure they assume that because, like I told you, I run the cops. The guineas will tear themselves apart figuring one of them must've plugged you and they'll set to killin' each other like they always do. I'll hang back, sit pretty and rip them off while they tire themselves out."

Kennedy looked at Quinn's gun and pressed himself even further against the wall. "But Siegel will know and…"

"He won't say shit on account of him not wanting to look weak in front of his pals." Doyle looked at the cringing Kennedy over the rim of the cup as he finished the last drop. "So you can either go on makin' money with me or you can die right here and now. You chose."

Kennedy jerked his quivering chin at Quinn's gun. "Put that away and we'll talk."

"No reason to put it away until we've agreed," Doyle said. "Do we agree?"

Kennedy balled his slender hand into a fist and slammed it back against the bedroom door. "God damn you for putting me in this position."

"Damn yourself." Doyle nodded to Quinn to aim the gun at Kennedy's head. "Last chance, Joey."

"Fine! Our agreement stands! I'll…"

Quinn pocketed the .45 just as the bedroom door cracked open and a woman's voice called Kennedy's name. "Joe? Is that you? What's all the ruckus about?"

Doyle poured on the charm. "That wouldn't be my good friend Gloria, would it?"

Quinn was surprised to see Gloria Swanson peak out from between the door and the door frame. She was so tiny and tan and looked much different in real life than in any of her movies. Even though her face was swollen from sleep, she still looked like a movie star. She smiled at Doyle and said, "Hey ya, Archie. What are you doing here? I tried getting Joe to take me to see you at the Longford Lounge tonight, but he said he had business."

"That so?" Doyle smiled at Kennedy who didn't smile back. "Well, I just had a few things to talk over with him, but you can have him back." He looked at Kennedy. "We're all square, right, Joey?"

"Sure. I'll handle everything, don't worry."

Doyle got up and signaled Quinn to do the same. "Why don't you let me handle that? I'll see to it they understand what happened."

Quinn could tell Kennedy didn't like it, but there wasn't much he could do about it now that his mistress was standing right there.

When Quinn stood up, he felt the actress's eyes move up and down and all around his body. "Who's your new friend, Archie. I don't think I've ever seen him before."

"That's Terry, my associate. Come by the Lounge tomorrow night and you'll see more of him."

Quinn felt himself blush as she eyed his broad shoulders. "Thanks, I think I will." She suppressed a yawn. "See you around, Archie."

Doyle blew her a kiss as he got up to leave. "See you around, honey." He winked at Kennedy. "You, too, Joey."

Quinn followed Doyle out of the room and into the hall. He rang for the elevator, but was surprised to see Kennedy had stepped out into the hallway after them "Enjoy it while it lasts, Doyle, because there's going to come a time when bastards like you won't be able to do something like this to me."

Doyle laughed as he put his hat on his head. "I wouldn't count on it. Nobody's big enough to stop a bullet, Joey, and a bullet's all it takes."

"Maybe in your world," Kennedy said, "but not in mine."

Doyle set his bowler on his head. "We'll see, Joey. We'll see. Love to Gloria." He winked again. "And Rose, of course."

Kennedy flushed, but the elevator arrived and he darted back to his room to keep the operator from seeing him.

Quinn let Doyle board first and told the operator to take them to the lobby.

It was a long trip down and Quinn knew Doyle hated silences. He wasn't surprised when his boss asked him, "Think he learned anything tonight?"

He'd always encouraged Quinn to speak his mind, so he did. "No. His kind never does until it's too late."

Doyle let out a long sigh as he watched the lights on the control panel show the elevator's descent. "No. No, they don't."

THE
Winners

by E.F. Schraeder

Brookline, Massachusetts 1930

"You think I don't see you, but I know you're there." Rose shook her head, and pulled the threaded needle up past her head. She sighed as the needle poked through the wool of her son's small, tailored coat. "I count the stitches," she said. She pulled the thread high then drove the needle into the thick fold of gray fabric again. "I secure it first." She held up a green toned button; peeking through its holes she saw her eldest daughter Rosie in a dark corner of the bedroom, her body half obscured by the buttonholes. A shadow covered half of the child's face. "You're only half here," her mother smiled.

Rain pelted the window until the shutters rattled. Rose looked up from her chair and spoke deliberately, "That downpour outside washes away our sins."

Rosie squirmed in the corner. She hated talk of sin. "Rubbish! It's for the flowers!" she chimed, her voice piercingly loud. She stomped her feet as she walked toward her mother.

Rose frowned. "Gentle steps for a lady," she corrected. Rose returned her eyes to the task. She lowered the button over the thread and released it. The button slipped easily over the thread, spinning as it fell before landing into place on the jacket.

Young Rosie watched it silently, as if she wondered where it would end up. Of course, it couldn't possibly go anywhere without the guidance of the thread. Rosie plopped herself onto the bed beside her brother. The bed creaked.

Rosie was a lean, lovely girl. Her mother smiled at her, then at Bobby, perched on the edge of his bed. His feet thumped on the oak frame mindlessly.

From a room below, a mantle clock chimed the hour. The bellowing song captured the children's surprise, their eyes big and round for a moment.

"Our old family clock scares you? Silly children," their mother pronounced, still stitching the flat, dark button carefully onto the small tweed jacket. "Maybe you think I should have better to do?" she asked them. They remained silent. "You're never too well off to tend to your own work," she said. "You'll see."

She stitched the knot tightly on the inside of the coat and snipped off the trail of thread. She flicked the newly fastened button with her forefinger to make sure it was secure. Both children still watched her carefully, as if she'd woven some bit of magic into Bobby's coat. "Next time, be careful with it, young man. No pulling off your buttons." She patted him on the head then added, "Or anyone else's."

Rosie frowned. She eyed their mother suspiciously. She hopped out of the corner and toward Bobby's dresser. "Why do you count the stitches?" she asked, leaning herself on the tall dresser. She swayed her charcoal colored wool skirt around her. The pleats danced like débutantes at a ball.

Rosemary stopped in the doorway. She held a small tan sewing bag in one hand and moved closer to the child, smiling. "To keep everything in place, of course. I count one for each of you, my pretty girl." She pinched the girl's cheek until it went pink.

Riverdale, New York, December 1940

"It's a bargain, Rose, really. With everything we have to lose," Joe said. "I only want winners in this family. You know that." His voice was low and controlled, but stern.

Rosie listened from the upstairs hall. She made herself small, hunched in a ball in the shadows. She didn't want to be seen. She wanted to listen. At twenty-two, she had every right to march downstairs and demand an audience, but curiosity got the better of her. Her parents' voices rumbled between frustration and anger. She peered between the rails of the staircase and saw them pacing in the foyer.

Her father stood at the mantle. Beside the clock sat a perfectly groomed miniature tree he tended carefully. He called it his "memento of the war." Rosie didn't follow quite what he meant by that, but it was pretty, all the same. Beside the tree he placed a row of dark candles on glistening silver plates. He lit candles, then her mother quickly blew them out. *What sort of funny game were they playing?*

"We can't ever know!" Mother raised her voice. "We can't know which one, or how, or what will become of them."

"But we have to ensure they have a chance to succeed. It's our responsibility. England is a bust. We need to build it here. Their inheritance demands it." His tone sounded scolding, finger wagging. "We owe it to them, Rose. They can change everything, you know it, with the power we're talking about."

Rose's face flattened. Her eyes suddenly looked cold and cruel.

Rosie blinked, wondered if the shadows played a trick on her mother's face.

Joe continued, "It's not what I want, Rose. It's the agreement. It was made before either of us had a choice, really. I'm the architect of this family." He set a hand on the small tree. "The design was handed to me, and we have to do our part before it's too late."

Rose brought her hands up to her face and turned away from him. She looked suddenly frazzled and afraid in the dim light of the room. She turned to him, nodding, "If it isn't already too late. We've got nine now, Joseph. How many can they take?"

Joseph walked to the mantle and cinched his fingertips closed around a candle flame. It extinguished with a hiss, and a flicker of smoke traced up between his fingers. His face remained expressionless as he gazed at his wife. "But it's not stock commodities we're trading, Rose," his voice low, scratchy.

"It isn't a Hollywood movie you're producing, either, Joe. You can't script their lives," she snapped.

Father looked like he'd been stung by something, like the shrill tone of mother's voice pierced him. He glared at his wife.

Rose pressed, "Why should we risk them?"

Rosie wondered. She suddenly felt nervous and clenched her breath in her mouth. She felt her stomach flip and jump, and pulled her legs up tight to her chest. Her heart thudded so loud in her ears that she thought she'd explode. She'd never seen her parents so upset. *And who were "they"?*

"And we just unleash it on them? Let others decide who to take?" Rose persisted. She ran her fingers through her thick hair.

"It's the only way to ensure one of them receives our position," Joe replied, his voice solid and stern.

"But the punishments are so severe."

"It's the price. It's been decided, Rose. By your father, Mr. Mayor, as much as by me. Try not to take it on. That's how I live with it," he said, clasping his hands. "Besides, you know what we have planned for young Joe. He's to be president. There has to be payment for that." His lips tightened around the words.

Rosie knew that much. She always liked how they talked about her brother before tonight. She watched while her parents stood in the dark, their hands together for a few moments.

Silently her father walked into the center of the room. He knelt down, drawing something on the floor with his finger. Rosie couldn't make out the figure clearly. Her mother picked up the candles and relit them, one at a time until the room glowed with the warmth of twinkling flames like stars on a clear night.

Rosie's mother walked toward him slowly in the dark, her face illuminated by the glow of the single purple candle she held. Her simple black dress swayed around her legs. *Mother was so elegant.*

But Rose's face remained serious and strained. "It isn't easy for me, Joe. They've come from me, too." She clenched her belly then reached out a hand and stroked Joseph's arm. She clung to his bicep and moved closer to him. His height seemed to swallow her delicate frame as he swept a lanky arm around her.

The intimacy of the moment forced Rosie to glance away from them. She didn't want to see her parents kiss. *How awful!* Her mother whispered into his ear and held the candle between them. She whispered something again, then he repeated it. Then mother spoke again, her voice low and throaty.

Rosie didn't understand the words, but she strained to hear. She didn't like it. Her face felt hot with an indeterminate anger, and her stomach ached. Rosie rubbed her eyes and stood up, quietly as she could. One of the old floorboards creaked under her feet as she stepped lightly down the hall, and she let out a slight gasp. She rushed back toward her room. She passed her brothers' rooms and felt relieved the doors were closed. *Maybe they hadn't heard anything?* She'd pretend she was asleep. She threw herself into bed and pulled up the blankets high to cover her face. She didn't want her parents to know she was eavesdropping. They were always so angry with her for her antics.

Rose swung the door open seconds later. She knew the girl heard everything, and she bit back a cry in her throat thinking of it: the eldest daughter, her namesake, a perfect likeness of herself as a young girl. A single tear crept down Rose's cheek as she watched the girl feign sleep. She wouldn't have long, her beautiful girl.

1941, Dr. Freeman's Care

"Count backwards from one hundred, Rosie," Dr. Freeman requested.

Rose's face fell slack. The doctor loomed over her, dangling his questions out like worms on the end of a fishing line. He pressed something toward her. The thin saw blade entered, a hum vibrated in her ears. She flinched but didn't cry. *Stay strong*, she told herself, thinking of her father. *He'd be proud.* The numbers blurred as the incision deepened. The doctor frowned severely, wiping a blood smeared glove on his white gown. *I wore a white gown once, didn't I?*

Rose sat in the foyer waiting for a call. She avoided the hospital. She didn't want to be there, to hear or see a moment of it. *After.* Joe hadn't even bothered to inquire if she would've agreed. Just decided. A scowl gripped her mouth and deep lines set in an expression that would become permanent.

She glanced up from the armchair and stared at Joe's tree. He'd clipped one of the lowest branches off last night, said it was unbalanced. Then this morning he called her to tell her what was happening, where he'd taken their child. She should have known.

Her body clenched, muscles knotted up and down her spine in anger. *How could he?* Though she knew something had to be done, she hated him for it. The weight of it settled onto her shoulders, though he'd done it. *He'd delivered poor Rose like a package to the post.* She bit down on her lip hard and listened to her fingernails click on the fine grain of the polished oak table beside her. *Waiting.*

The telephone ring interrupted her reverie of vitriol. She picked up the receiver and took in the information he delivered. She swallowed hard and prayed. Rosie would never be the same. She knew that much. And she'd never forgive any of it. She clenched her jaw and allowed the yearning to pass. She held herself in perfect stillness and accepted that the struggle was over.

1944, The Family War

Joe's hopes were pegged onto a shooting star that went dim. Junior's heroism was rewarded with a posthumous Naval Cross. *A bitter reward.* Father frowned, traced his hand along the line of his namesake's casket. He peered at Rose, wondering if she knew better than he how to wear the loss. He wouldn't cry, wouldn't weaken himself that way. *No crying allowed.* That was the rule. But it broke him to lose that boy. Even hovering over the casket he pushed himself to think of the next move, the next win.

"It's up to Jack, now." Joe's face showed the strain of the loss, lines deep and eyes dark.

"I know," Rose confirmed, her hands clasped tight on her lap. They'd have their winner. She bit the inside of her cheek gently, allowed the moment of reckoning to settle. "But it isn't who he is, Joe. He's a writer. A camera hog and a playboy." Protective urges swelled in her chest.

"He just hasn't prepared for it, that's all. Spends his days frolicking in the sun. He's got to learn it now." Rose nodded, but remained silent. Joe added, "We'll sell him like soap flakes."

A familiar frown settled on Rose's face.

When Jack announced his bid for the U.S. House of Representatives a few short years later, it landed without much familial celebration. It was less a surprise than a request for salt across the Sunday dinner table.

"It's a necessary step," Joe said, smiling at his fine son. *He'd win. He had to win.* It was better than luck, it was destiny.

Jack swallowed the next few years of milestones like pain killers, and after, the U.S. Senate race fell into place. He knew what was next.

December, 1961

Rose splurged for a suitable mourning dress and prepared for a serious and historic funeral. But the old man recovered from the stroke, at least partly.

Unable to walk, unable to talk, how's that feel for the architect? Rose wondered. She hung the dress up in the large closet and draped a plastic bag over it. She'd use it soon enough.

But the weight of father's demise sank the rest of the family like the Titanic. Jack and Bobby tried to keep up a strong front when they went to see him, plastering bright smiles on their handsome faces. But the room felt too closed and stale. And neither of them liked seeing their father stuck in that damned chair. *The indignity of it. Such a great man.*

The playboy son became a legend, and JFK's milestones swelled Joe with pride. The establishment of a Peace Corp was nice, then there was handling the Berlin Wall, and avoiding a third world war. That was something. To top it all off, they sent an American into space. *The playboy had his wrinkles, but it all panned out nicely, hadn't it?*

On another dreary visit to Dad, Jack's back stiffened in the chilly chair, sending shooting pains down his leg. After the dim visit, President Jack clasped his brother's arm sadly and said, "Old age is a shipwreck." It was a truth he didn't want to face. And wouldn't.

◇ ◇ ◇ ◇ ◇

Ted ran and won in the Massachusetts Senate. Joe smiled, observing the truth behind the scandal of a college dismissal as innuendo. *Winners only.*

Joe watched the news, kept score, and tallied his bets. In 1963, he looked broken, but kept himself alive with the hope he planted in the next son. Everyone always loved Bobby.

After the November '63 disaster in Texas, Bobby felt the burden sink into his wanting heart. His wife Ethel adored him, his children loved him, and people across the United States worshiped him with a frenzy worthy of Elvis or one of the Beatles. He missed his brother, but believed he could do some good. His family seemed to have a lot to give. He decided to pick up the family sport. A New York Senate seat was his, practically an inheritance. *Why not?* Crowds thudded their praise during moving speeches, barely able to hear the solemnity of his message over the surging public approval. Bobby believed. It was his turn.

Rosemary's Lobotomy

by James Frederick William Rowe

"Our father
Lord in Heaven
Hallowed by thy name
Bykinggssdumco
byllbe…"
We've gone far enough

Rosemary Kennedy
A pretty, charming child
But sadly slow
She liked Winnie the Pooh
And writing in her journal
She did not do much else

She has become so troublesome
Sneaking from the nuns
Would that she were still a child
She was not so bad then
But as she grows
She becomes worse: What can we do?

(continued)

She met the king and queen
Practicing for hours
To properly greet them
She did splendidly
Until she tripped
She does not seem to remember that part

Underneath the upper eyelid
The instrument goes
Originally an ice pick, and now not much different
Twisted to cut through the grey matter
Then driven in further again
"Rosemary, dear, recite the Lord's Prayer for us?"

Canvassing the Vote

by John Hayes

Kennedys at my windows
rattling on the frames
begging for my vote,

A cyclone whips across the night
roofs and cows whirl in the sky
trees uproot and smash the ground.
Zeus is blown from Mt. Olympus.
The turtle swims away.
Apollo's chariot on his back.
"Not to worry," Kennedy promises.
 "I can rise and set the sun
but first I need your vote."

In the morning I gather limbs
chainsaw my fallen tree.
Watch Kennedy ride the sun across the sky.
Worry that when he gets to Vegas
he'll lose the sun
and darkness will prevail.

GOIN' TO
THE MOON

by James William Frederick Rowe

"We choose to go to the Moon
In this decade and do other things
Not because they are easy
But because they are hard"
What? No.
It's not about that at all!
It's not about rising to
Meet the challenge
Of some noble enterprise
It's about that son of a bitch
Man on the Moon
Eyeballin' us for millennia
Starin' down from on-high
Goadin' us
Makin' us look the fool
Sayin' "Can't get to me!"

And those God damned Reds
Thinkin' "We'll show those
Capitalist pigs
And start importing
Moon cheese to all the comrades

To feed the Mother Russia of tomorrow"
Will we lose to some vodka-swilling
Socialist sluggards?
Hell no!

We will get to the Moon
Not because it is easy
But because we want to
Stomp a mudhole in the Man in the Moon's ass
And rub it in some Ruskie face while we're there!

Good speech, though.

TWO BROTHERS FIGHTING

by Jack Horne

two brothers fighting
      over the same femme fatale
           Marilyn Monroe
                likes the besotted Bobby
                    but adores President John

MARILYN'S VOWS

by Patricia Bruce

Dearest Jack:

The plummeting of us begins and
ends in the aftermath of your
desires

Perhaps our whispers pierce
political gain, perhaps our trysts
plunder family shelter

Politics aside, now I'm wallowing,
feeling undone,
toppled, you might say

But it was your heart's final goodbye that rippled my love thru
crass emotions

Now Springtime's movie scene
slips unseen between
my fragile fingers

(continued)

I'm left with flowers shorn, petals
smeared, music stilled
and Bobby's genius cannot heal

Always yearning the spirit of your love,
I treasure your empty vows
as we part

Love forever, Marilyn

A LONELY ACTRESS

by Jack Horne

a lonely actress
phones her married lover—
Marilyn is dead

OUT OF FRAME

by Jarrid Deaton

It's 1963 and William Greer punches the gas while blood and skull fragments fly from the shattered head of an important man slumped in the back seat of the Lincoln convertible. The man's wife fell from the car a mile or so back, lunging for her husband, hysterics short-circuiting her balance and movement. Greer's sudden acceleration sent her somersaulting over the trunk to the pavement where she broke her wrist and received a moderate case of road rash.

A man named Zapruder, his receptionist helping him hold the camera. A star gone supernova and then nothing, caught on film. Frame 210. Frame 313. One then two. Neck. Head.

Stopping the car means solemn voices on radio waves and mournful faces relaying tragic news on the television.

Tires continuing to gather miles means something else, although Greer admits to himself that he isn't sure what the end result will be, or the importance of the part he is playing.

The Lincoln is being followed by police and line after line of dark cars, but they keep their distance. The dying man spills life all over the leather. Greer knows he should drive to a hospital, or stop and let the authorities handle the situation, but the man is only dead when they have his body. He also knows that he himself is an authority, that he was chosen for this specific task of transportation, so he adds a new selection to the list of options.

Punch the gas. Drive.

CAMELOT

by James Penha

I had begged my parents to say goodbye at the Howard Johnson's where we lunched and not, please, not to escort me to the campus where, I knew, most new students would have driven their own cars. It was going to be hard enough to be a sixteen-year old college freshman, too young for a driver's license, not man enough to have to shave, naïve in the ways of the world despite growing up in New York City, without having my parents carry me over the threshold of my dorm room.

"You're going to lug those two huge duffles all the way by yourself? Don't be silly, Willie." How I loathed that rhyme!

My father concurred. "Your mother's right. As usual. We'll drop you off." I unsheathed the frankfort I was eating and smashed its roll on the table. The hot dog hung from my mouth like a flaccid cigar. "But we'll be discreet. No displays of affection. Or grief." He turned to my mother. "Right, hon?"

"Like taxi drivers. You can pay us if you want."

But, of course, as we left HoJo's, my mother grabbed me and kissed my forehead with such force I stumbled backwards into the revolving doors and was turned out of the restaurant. I stalked off to our station wagon and waited for my father to unlock the car. Sliding into the back seat, I said, when my mother had found the grooves of her place near the driver, "Student Affairs Building. And step on it."

After a half-hour wait in a long corridor queue, I dragged my bags to the desk of a residence assistant who asked for my name and ID number. According to a name tag, he was Drew, an MBA candidate. "Okay, here's your key. You're in Room 327 of Pershing Hall. That's on the third floor, of course. If you look at the map on the back wall there, you'll find out how to get there. You have a car, right?"

"Uh, no. I...I took a taxi to get here...from the train station."

"That your luggage?" We both looked down at the bulbous canvas sacks at my feet. I nodded. "Ouch. It's about a half-mile from here. You'll see a star on the map. That's here, where you are now. Good luck. At least you have a cool roommate," he added as I bent for the bags.

"Really?"

"Sean Kennedy." The assistant grinned. I didn't know how to react.

"He's cool?"

"He's a Kennedy."

"A Kennedy?"

"A Kennedy. Of the Kennedys? THE Kennedys."

"I never heard of a Sean Kennedy," I said with some vehemence. Although I couldn't claim to be an expert on the President's clan, from the time he was nominated in Los Angeles, I had kept a scrapbook of every mention and photograph of JFK I could clip from the *Daily News* (my parents' morning tabloid), the *Long Island Press* (delivered to our house each evening), and on school days the *Herald-Tribune* (which I ordered in home room instead of the *Times*, just to be different), and from any magazine I could tear away and up from anyone's house. After the election, the scrapbook extended into a second and then multiple volumes. I kept track of every appointment to the cabinet, every plan for the New Frontier. Not only the text of the inaugural address, but a 45rpm EP recording of the speech. The Peace Corps. Ireland. "I'm the man who accompanied Jacqueline Kennedy to Paris." Ich bin ein Berliner. Cuba—the Bay of Pigs in '61 and those days in October 1962 when Mr. Pollack, my high school science teacher, said he didn't much feel like talking about nuclear physics and read us "The Laughing Man" instead—had a volume all its own. As did the personal and family matters: Jackie, Caroline, John-John, baby Patrick. *Life's* photos of

JFK in swim trunks greeting beach-goers in Florida or the tabloid pix of the President half-naked on the beach at Hyannis or amidst relatives on one or another craft were enclosed in plastic-covered pages. I would have remembered a Sean.

"I don't think he's a nephew, more like a second or third cousin I think. At least that's what I hear."

"I can't imagine any Kennedy cousin having to live in a dorm."

"Mandatory for freshmen. You should know that." I didn't. Since my financial aid package included room and board, I hadn't considered any option other than living on campus. "Mandatory— no exceptions. It's a rule."

"Right." After signing a raft of contractual obligations, I grabbed a key, thanked Drew, tugged on the duffels, and followed the map to arrive at an elevatorless Pershing Hall. By the time I opened the door of 327, I was soaked with sweat. The room was simply appointed with two closets, two beds, two desks, two dressers. It wasn't completely square—the desks were in a little nook under a huge window with a view of the quadrangle. There was no bathroom. The freshman dormitory had two toilet/shower rooms, one on either end of each floor. I figured the commodes would have some privacy, but feared that there would only be community showers. At sixteen, my genitalia was unimpressive, as my only slightly older cousin Bill had loudly pointed out a few months earlier, when we were changing for a dip in the lake near my uncle's house. "You're still fucking bald." It wasn't literally true, and things had improved a bit since then, but I spent an enormous amount of time, as college approached, worrying about how I would hide my immaturity, even practicing showering in a bathing suit. I was ready to explain that my religion, Islam, was very strict about public nudity. I was really Catholic, but fortunately circumcised in case anyone did catch a glimpse of my penis while I was peeing or something. If anyone asked about the tenets of my faith, I thought I would be pretty safe inventing them. No one in America knew anything about Moslems. And if there were any Arabs in the dorm, I was ready to switch adherence to a conservative Protestant sect found mostly in East Timor, which is where, I would say, my grandmother came from.

It seemed by the pair of Coach bags leaning against one of the beds that Sean was already in residence, but I hesitated to sit on the other bed for fear he hadn't rejected it, but had only carelessly dropped his luggage. I collapsed on one of the desk chairs when the door opened, and a tall, broad young man entered, his tousled reddish brown hair dripping from a recent shower. His chest was tanned copper beneath a delicate filagree of fur. Clad in a white terry towel, he smiled broadly as he strode over to grab and shake my trembling hand. "William Livingston, I presume. Great to meet you, Bill. I'm Sean."

"Willie, actually. Will, really. William Livingstone."

"Sounds like someone is having an identity crisis." He laughed at his own joke. Towering over me by at least a foot, he set his hands on my shoulders. "But that's what college is for. Will, we are going to be great friends."

Letting me go, he peeled the towel. I tried not to stare, but he was the first naked man I had ever seen, and he was so very naked and so very manly. My father might actually have been from an East Timorese sect, so reticent was he to show off his body, and Joey Goldstein, my friend from around the block who taught me the facts of life by jerking us both off under a blanket in the back seat of his grandmother's parked car, had equipment more practiced but only slightly more adult than my own

If I hadn't been thoroughly perspired already, I would have been then.

Sean was in no rush to get dressed. He sprawled on what I now understood was his chosen bed by his bags and told me what he had learned about the campus, the dorm, and the students on our floor, gesturing demonstratively as he imitated this English major and that would-be accountant. His dramatizations were wonderful, and soon I was on the floor, grabbing my stomach, hysterical.

"What's your field, Will?"

"Pre-Med."

"Fah out!" He continued, "Bio, Physics, Chem, Analytic Geometry and Calculus? No time to get laid unless you find the perfect test tube."

"What's your major?"

"Political Science. Funny really. They call it a science, but there are no test tubes in politics. It's an aht."

"Huh?"

"It's an aRt," he revised his pronunciation.

"Right." Oh, how I was tempted to ask from whom he had learned that. And where he got that accent. But I didn't want to skew up the start of what might be a genuine friendship. And besides, that chest, so much like JFK's in *Life* and that hair, the same hue that had so shocked me when I saw the candidate campaigning in my New York neighborhood the day before the election. Whether or not Sean was one of THE Kennedys, he was good enough for me.

It was an hour or more before Sean got into his boxers and asked if I would be going to the orientation mixer in the Student Union that night. "I don't think so. I'm pretty tired from the trip…"

"Hey, come on. It's a good way to check out the ladies, Will. Not to mention finding some more frosh to imitate. Hey, Will, do it for me, okay? I hate to go into a room without a friend."

I agreed, and turned my back to him to put on my bathing suit and towel before heading for the showers. If he found it odd, or if he even attended to this odd ritual of mine, Sean never said so.

And I never commented on Sean's idiosyncrasies, like his penchant for nudity while in our room or his puffing on his little cigars at the corner of our big window, or his bringing an array of co-eds to his bed where, whether I was out at the library or at my desk studying organic chem, the sex proceeded in a variety of positions I wish I could have described to Joey Goldstein.

President Kennedy's sexual appetite was hardly common knowledge in 1963, but my Aunt Blanche, cousin Bill's mother, repeated, whenever I enthused over JFK, what she had heard from a bellboy at the Carlyle Hotel in Manhattan: that its Presidential Suite was reserved permanently for John Kennedy's adulterous liaisons.

I refused to believe Blanche. Until I met Sean.

There were times I played interference for Sean, for instance when he was being sucked by a senior in his bed, while the Registrar's secretary was whispering for him at our door. I never minded.

On the rare nights he neither spent out nor in with a woman, he would, after finishing his reading for next day's classes, set the textbooks in a careful pile on his desk, take the latest *Playboy* from a drawer and lean it, open to the centerfold, against the pile, ease back in his chair, shuffle off his pants, and masturbate, breathing and stroking himself with increasing ardor. The first time this happened, he said, without turning from his ardor, "Willie, I hope you don't mind. Every guy our age does this, right? No reason to hide, really, is there? Especially from a friend, yeah?"

"No, of course not." I meant it. I never wanted Sean to hide from me. Especially this. If he wondered why I never jerked off in front of him or why I never allowed him to see my dick, he never asked. He had no reason to care.

When he came, he did so with a roar to match the force of the ejaculation. Then he turned, with his great toothy smile, shook the sweat from his face, grabbed a towel, and made for the showers. In the five minutes of his absence, I would open my fly and, closing my eyes to a montage of rampant Kennedys, relieve myself into a Kleenex.

I did well in my classes, earning almost straight As, and so I must have put in a lot of time reading and studying and working in the labs. I got the part of Happy in the Drama Club's production of *Death of a Salesman* scheduled to open for a weekend in late November with rehearsals almost every evening for the six weeks before. But if lingering memories are in any way a gauge of spent time, my life then was clocked with Sean Kennedy as Proust's life was devoted to madeleines. If I wasn't actually with Sean I was on a mission for him: detouring to the student center to Xerox the pages of a library book he needed or picking up a pack of rubbers. I was his Kenny O'Donnell, and he was my Kennedy. I'd find films and campus events for us to go to based on what I came to understand were his preferences: gymnastic meets, Hitchcock movies, jazz. The swagger I gave to Hap Lowman I borrowed from Sean, and I hoped he'd notice my impersonation when he attended opening night.

I had a Bio Lab that finished at four in the afternoon before the Friday debut, so it would be something of a rush to pick up a snack at the canteen, walk to the theatre, do my makeup, don my costume, and meditate my way into Happyness before the seven o'clock curtain. But as I paid for my sandwich at the canteen, the cashier asked, "So did you hear?"

"Hear what?"

"The president was shot!"

"Someone shot the president of the University?"

"Jesus, no. The President! Kennedy!"

"The President?"

"If he recovers, he'll be unbeatable next year."

I ran as fast as I could to the dorm, paused to catch a second wind at the stairwell, and climbed, panting, to our room. Sean wasn't there. I had seen most of the residents in the common room on the first floor when I arrived, and so returned there. But Sean was not among the crowd. No one had seen him. There were a few comments about his surname and rumors of his relationship to the first family, but most of the talk was about the assassination. The President was dead.

There was no run left in me, but I walked as quickly as I could to the theatre. The whole cast and crew was seated in the orchestra trying to decide if the opening should be delayed. Maureen, our director, was crying. "It's not just a show-must-go-on thing, I'm saying. What else are we going to feel like doing tonight?"

"But no one is going to go out to see a play now. There will be no one in the audience," said Beth, our Linda.

"So it will be another dress rehearsal." There was nothing else to say. "Okay?" There was nothing else to do really.

Five or six people did show up with tickets. They saw an amazing production of *Death of a Salesman*. Never had we better felt the fragility of the American Dream as we did that night.

I didn't bother to remove my make-up after the curtain call, but ran back to our dorm room. No Sean.

I showered as discretely as ever. No Sean.

We had been best friends for ten weeks, but our relationship had black holes as well as novae. Because I had never wanted to let him think I cared for him because he was related to the President, I never asked him if he was related to the President. Corollary black holes followed. I didn't ask about his parents or where he lived or what his home phone number was.

And so I lay on Sean's bed and cried for the death of a president. Classes were canceled for the rest of the weekend, as were the remaining performances of *Death of a Salesman*. Maureen said we'd reschedule the show at the beginning of the next term since the following weekend was Thanksgiving with final exams following hard upon the holiday.

It wasn't until I entered our room after sitting for my Chem final, that I again saw Sean. Slumped at his desk, he raised his head and attempted a smile, but there wasn't much smile in it.

"You came back for exams?"

"No, I'm not prepared. I'm taking a leave of absence before I fail everything. That way I can come back in good standing if I ever want to."

"You're leaving—?" I choked on the unsaid me.

"Yeah, I'm a terrific freshman, but not much of a student, you know?"

There was a long silence.

"Hungry? I'll make an A&W run. Up for a hot dog and root beer?"

"Yeah, sure. Great. Thanks, Will."

When I returned with dinner, Sean was stretched out on the floor in his boxer shorts. I dared to strip to my jockeys, sat opposite, and spread a picnic in between us. We didn't talk much, not about the President, of course, but not even about my play…because it would have required us to talk about the President. Mostly, we grasped at shared memories.

I cleaned up the trash and sat next to Sean. "I'll…I'll miss you, man."

"Yeah, I know. Same here."

We sat.

"Willie? Will you do me a favor?"

"Sure. What?"

He slipped off his boxers. "Would you mind?" He quickly nodded his head toward his lap. "I'm in no mood for visitors, and I…you don't have to…" He moved to get to his bed.

"No. No. I don't mind. Joey Goldstein and I used to do it all the time when we were kids." I grabbed his dick and felt it harden. "It's …it's just a circle jerk. We're…a circle…"

"Jerk!" Sean smiled, leaned back against his bed and closed his eyes. When his familiar groans signaled his orgasm was on the way, I enveloped him with my mouth and swallowed the spring of his dynasty.

"Hey, Will. That was, uh, nice actually."

"You're welcome," I mumbled stupidly.

We crawled to our beds and slept.

Sean blinked open his eyes momentarily when the clock alarmed me for the morning's Analytical Geometry exam, but he was snoring by the time I eased out of the door. When I returned for lunch, Sean and his stuff were gone.

From time to time, now, I Google "Sean Kennedy". There are thousands of results. I have yet to find my Sean or any Sean related to President Kennedy, not among the top hits I have bothered to click anyway.

I have told this story to a few good friends over the years. Of course, they ask if Sean was really related to JFK. To most I admit I don't know. Only to some do I say that he was.

A PATSY?

---

by Jack Horne

A patsy? Oswald was charged with the crime;
His killer, Ruby, expired doing time…

HANNAH'S
DARLING

by Anna Sykora

The day she moved in with us, in the back of the Eldorado Towers, Hannah hung a framed photo of JFK above her bed. Smooth-faced and thick-haired, bracketed at his desk by a pair of American flags, he gazed down with a glint of amusement at the cards of saints she taped to her battered dresser. He'd just taken office in 1961.

In those fairy tale days of rent control, we paid 365 dollars a month for nine rooms with no view of Central Park. Hannah earned 65 dollars a week, I believe, plus room and board. Her snug room, next to our washer and dryer, the window looking out on a bare, brick wall, was painted sunny yellow to make her feel at home. My sister and I, aged 6 and 8, had already sent two housekeepers packing.

When Mother begged the agency for one "with a firmer hand," we got Hannah Kelly, sturdy as a boxer in shapeless, woolly clothes and shoes like a nun's. Her wide face fringed with coarse, grey hair that looked as if she cut it herself, her eyes a no-nonsense blue, Hannah arrived toting one suitcase and a copy of *The Daily News.*

"She has no teeth," Mother warned us. "There aren't enough dentists in Ireland. Now I want you girls to behave, for a change. I'm wrecking my health to earn her salary." (A psychotherapist with patients in the entertainment biz, Mother worked from 2 PM till after midnight; so we mostly saw her on the weekends. As for our dad, he mostly hid downtown at Lincoln Towers, with his girlfriend.)

"Is it true you've got no teeth?" I hissed on Hannah's first morning trying to get us ready for school. Stirring oatmeal in a double boiler, she just pushed out her dentures with her tongue, and Penny and I ran away shrieking. Still stirring the pot, I suppose, Hannah stood her ground and whinnied like a horse.

She soon got the upper hand, slapping mine whenever I talked back. If Penny and I didn't finish our plates—and hot, filling food we got for a change, with meat and potatoes and heaps of greens—she threatened to keep us on bread and water.

The three of us ate at the yellow formica table in the kitchen. One evening Hannah scolded: "Nina, do you think your nourishment grows on trees?" I'd never thought about it, not beyond the Broadway Supermarket. "In Ireland we take a bit of bread to sop up this nice gravy." She showed us how, and then wiped her mouth on her sleeve.

Soon Penny imitated Hannah's sayings, crying for help from St Anthony when she couldn't find the precious doll I'd dumped out the fifth floor window out of spite. My curly-haired, adorable, plump little sister would sit at the kitchen table with Hannah, helping her fill the supermarket savings stamps into booklets to redeem. I wouldn't help, and Hannah told me I had a bad character. At school I kept to myself; at home I'd quarrel with Penny or curl up with a book.

Nothing got a rise out of Hannah, I found: not shooting suction-cup arrows onto the ceilings; not strewing clothes or toys around; not dropping my homework into the tub. Nothing, except my salty mouth. When I called Penny a shit-baked pig, Hannah blushed red as a fire engine:

"And what would President Kennedy say if he heard you swearing like a sailor?"

"I don't give a rat's ass," I retorted. Hannah grabbed me by the ear, marched me down the hall and through the laundry, and into her phone booth of a bathroom, where she sat me down on the toilet seat. Hugging me there while I squirmed and sputtered, she scrubbed out my mouth with Ivory soap.

"You've got no right," I sobbed, blowing bubbles.

"It's for your own good, you little heathen. Where's the nice lad who will marry you if you prance around cursing like a drunken sailor?"

Giggling in the doorway, my treacherous sister shouted, "How does it taste?"

"Like shit."

Hannah gave me a shake, grabbed the bar of soap and repeated her Christian duty: "And now, pert missy, how does it taste?"

"Like...*soap.*"

That sour taste lingers in my memory; still I don't feel angry at Hannah Kelly, who was only trying to make me good. And nobody paid her a dime for that.

She taught us how to fold up sweaters and rip the worn-out clothing into rags. I never saw her sitting, doing nothing; watching TV (she loved the soap operas, or any news starring JFK), she'd knit rapidly and deftly, turning out scarves and sweaters and socks like a machine.

Pumping a pedal Singer in the sunny corner of the dining room, she patiently sewed us all our smocks for school. These we wore with knee socks and turtlenecks, to the amusement of girls whose mothers picked out their clothes on Fifth Avenue; but I have to admit we didn't miss many days of school for sickness anymore. If we started to cough, Hannah dosed us with eggnogs or a "potion" of lemon juice and honey.

If she ever got a moment to herself, after doing all our sewing, cleaning, cooking and washing up, she'd sit at the yellow formica table, pasting photos of JFK into an album with covers of pink leatherette. Under each one she wrote the date in block letters, the only way I ever saw her write.

One sweltering day (the kitchen fan was broken) I complained: "Why do you bother cutting all these photos out of *The Daily News*? You could collect stamps like my uncle. Some are pretty, with birds and flowers."

"And what would I do with your old stamps, Nina?" I spied a twinkle in Hannah's blue eyes. "This president is young and handsome, and Irish. Not like that old stick, Eisenhower. What more could a woman want?"

Prodding for a sore spot, I pursued: "Well, Hannah, why didn't you ever get married?"

"I never had the time," she said crisply, with a little flinch that soothed my malice. Snipping Khrushchev out of a photo, she stuffed the bald Russian in the garbage can, and then pasted a grinning JFK down on a fresh page in her album, as if she'd captured a precious butterfly.

At night she prayed for the president's health. Penny, stealing cookies from the kitchen, listened at Hannah's door.

"Does she ever say anything about us?" I asked my sister.

"I don't know. Are we little heathens?"

"Probably."

"Then she wants more patience."

"Hannah has plenty," I conceded. "More than Mother, or my teachers."

"Hannah is good because she never gets the chance to be bad," said Penny wisely, and stuffed another Pepperidge Farm cookie into her mouth.

◊ ◊ ◊ ◊ ◊

In May of 1962 the Hollywood stars offered JFK a birthday salute, televised from old Madison Square Garden. Since Mother was out of town, having an affair with her divorce attorney, Hannah let us stay up and watch the show.

Bored, Penny fell asleep on the rug, pillowed on her teddy bear, and I don't remember much. Not till Marilyn Monroe came rushing onstage, glowing like a fuzzy angel. When she tossed away her white mink stole, I thought for a heartbeat she was naked. That flimsy, flesh-colored dress sparkled from the neck to the hem, as if dipped in diamonds.

"Mary, Jesus and Joseph." Hannah dropped her knitting on the floor. "You young girls shouldn't see this! That sinful creature isn't wearing any knickers." Lurching to her feet, she turned off the TV, almost knocking it off the stand; so we didn't get to hear the singer's breathy, scandalous, let's-make-love-right-here rendition of "Happy Birthday." (These days you can catch it on YouTube, preserved forever like the Zapruder film.) Without another word, Hannah bundled us into our nightgowns and packed us into our beds.

The next day, JFK's portrait was missing from over her bed. You could still see the sunny square it kept clean. Painted walls darken fast in New York City.

At the time, I didn't understand why Hannah blamed him for Marilyn Monroe's revealing dress (auctioned by Sotheby's in 1998 for over a million dollars).

I never again saw Hannah bending over her precious scrap book of JFK's pictures. Maybe she threw it in the garbage. Or maybe she dumped it out the window, like my mother dumped my father's favorite loafers. After the Cuban missile crisis, my parents finally got a divorce.

Hannah stayed on with us faithfully, running the house and cooking and cleaning, while our disheveled mother—now addicted to pep pills—worked ever longer hours. My sister had friends and got good grades. I felt my father had abandoned me. Angry and depressed, I chewed on paper and pencils and couldn't concentrate. If I failed every subject, nobody would say a word, I thought; I'd wind up in public school and get stabbed in the hall. So much the better.

Hannah made me show her my grades, however, and hounded me to do my homework, paying me in Pepperidge Farm cookies when I got a decent grade. If I failed she'd slap my hand, lamenting:

"This is a lazy, bad-natured hand. Nina, you can read books; you should try harder. Do you want to end up cleaning houses, and minding other people's brats?"

Hannah had gained half a body of weight, and the corners of her faded mouth turned down. She never told us tales of the leprechauns anymore before putting us to bed.

I remember one evening of the president visiting Ireland on TV. The people there gave him an astronaut's welcome, their faces glowing with love and joy. Standing at the ironing board behind me, while I tried to hem a skirt like she taught me, suddenly Hannah gave a painful sigh.

"What is it?" I asked quietly.

"Nina, that's Patrick Street in Cork you're seeing. That's just a few blocks from where I was born."

Throngs of well-wishers swarmed JFK's vehicle, frantically waving American flags. Many were hanging out of their windows, as if they didn't care if they fell. Anybody could have taken a pot shot at the president, then and there. They didn't, though: they worshiped this first son of Ireland ever to rise to such prestige.

Hannah wiped away a tear with her finger. Maybe she was feeling sick for home, or maybe she had a premonition.

She left us at the end of 1963, to take a job at a luxury hotel on the opposite side of Central Park. Mother said Hannah said she had a black nightmare, the kind whose warning you can't ignore: she saw our family drowning in a great flood…

She never waited to say goodbye, and I'm sure my sister and I would have cried. When we got back from Christmas, parked with Mother's mother in Albany, Hannah was simply gone.

◊ ◊ ◊ ◊ ◊

That November though, while I wallowed in bed with the math book I loathed, Hannah came barging in, wringing her hands, her blue eyes damp and swollen. She'd been sewing at the Singer machine; the TV still was clamoring.

"What happened?" I cried. "Did you hurt yourself?"

She sat down hard on the end of my bed, almost dislodging me. "Nina, they've shot the president." Was this the end of the world?

The room grew darker, and to my surprise Hannah seemed to be bouncing up and down. A racing heart can derange your vision.

"How's that?" I choked out.

"I don't know. My darling's dead and gone." She shed more tears, like bleeding from a wound, and I started to weep from shock or sympathy. I'd never seen her cry.

"Please don't, Hannah," I mumbled. "I promise to pass my math exam." (Did I? I can't remember; but it's Hannah who taught me to persist).

"Oh, this is a terrible thing, Nina, the worst there ever was in this world. Oh why, oh why did they take my dear so soon?"

Holy Day

by Liz Dolan

Prim in my proper dress, I sat
seventh period, red-lining Latin roots:

amo-amiable, rex-regalia. The November sun
blanched the library's tomes as Lincolnesque

Mr. Stollmeyer listed in, pale as parchment.
The president has been shot, he said.

We fingered our mouths as if testing
for breath How will we tell our students?

It was the feast of St. Cecelia, patroness
of music, pewter harp in hand. Forced

to marry, she remained a virgin, converted
Valerian. Unwilling to worship Roman idols

she was thrown into a vat of boiling oil
for burying bodies of believers rather than

let the vultures peck out their souls
dice their livers like dreck. Unlike Jack,

(continued)

she escaped unscathed, sweet notes floating
from her throat like swallows. I wonder if

the witty, handsome Jack could sing, recite
his Latin declensions, say his evening prayers. Once,

playing chicken, he cycled headlong into his brother
Joe, flew into the air, floated—until the whoosh,

the blow to the head, sharp, surprising and painful.
Relax, he told himself, twenty-eight stitches woven

into his shock of wheat-colored hair. Too late for stitches
now. His father told him he had the goods. My mother

always said, No good comes to those who warm their hearth
by peddlin' poteen. The siren of the fire engine

roaring by muffled the message on the loudspeaker.

ODE TO
O's CLOTHES

by Sarah Delap U

Horror is a handbag
of silk lining and suede
capitalized by Gucci.

You are the world's woman
next to the most powerful man
who has ruined your pillbox hat.

what now? You will not be trodden
upon,
you have design in your toes
and your sunglasses transform
every corn-husking whitewashed girl
in middle country.

Take this opportunity to wed

your love of the stylish and macabre
buy into the family, the mix
as smooth as lamb leather.

Do not become plagued by lesser materials
the band has left the stage
the team has left the arena
the government has abandoned the Capitol

(continued)

but the runway remains strong, strode upon
by your disciples and emulators alike.

The road ahead is full of spilled thread
a frayed edge
a sartorial crux.

But O., you are a Special K girl
by whatever means
necessary:
chemical, natural or homicidal
you will reach the apex of forgetting

slaughter the wool suit

to be duly remembered, your satin shirt and soul rendered

still.

THE NIGHT KENNEDY GOT SHOT

by Atar Hadari

I had a party that night. You believe it?
I had this place—early 60s, Michigan—
a whole basement—seventy five dollars a month,
and I invited everybody to these things—
Professors, undergraduates, bikers—it was too late to cancel—
And they came. The night Kennedy got shot. A meaner bunch
of vicious drunks I never saw in my entire life—
there were fist fights—strings of blood down my refrigerator—
prune juice poured in the fish-tank.
Called the police myself at 2am, had the bums thrown out—
only time in my life.
And these two or three stayed in my kitchen—
helped me pick up glass off the floor,
mop the toilet bowl clear of vomit;
then we sat around and wondered why Lee Oswald did it.
It was three am. We were past drunk.
Michigan dawn was five hours away
especially November—it was black out;
light on the beach probably didn't turn to grey
just went from pitch black to bruise to soiled gold
as if there wasn't anything between
night and that hung over day.
We drank warm beer. (The fridge had to be disconnected
to be cleaned.) We watched dawn on the water
still not knowing why Lee Oswald did it.

(continued)

I asked them all to go away. When one was left finally
alone at the kitchen door
there was light all over the harbour
like an egg was spilled on the kitchen floor,
"He was ready to go," he said, or something.
I disagreed. He wasn't ready to go—
you go when the wind says it's time to go,
that's when you go. I say
these many years later, there's a plan
for how the world works,
so when dawn rose over Lake Michigan,
there was a plan, just like how Kennedy lost his brains
all over the back of the Lincoln and—seconds later—
there were phones ringing all over Washington.
I don't know if you remember—some of you—most of you—
Christ—you weren't born—
but that morning it was pretty obvious
somebody somewhere knew how to get what they want.
And when you go into their garden
you probably don't find a flower that's not bruised
and under the tracks left by the worm holes
even the roots of the grass are frozen solid with the cold.

Salute

by James Frederick William Rowe

The young son salutes
A father's casket horse led
Grieving November

BOBBY'S CLOSE SHAVE

by Harri B. Cradoc

"You know I don't like it when you guys smoke in here," was all Joey could think to say. But then he went on cutting hair as if nothing had happened.

A big man reading *U.S. News & World Report* took a cigar out of his mouth and studied it. "Excuse me, Joey, but it's something of a holiday around here and I'm feeling like I need to light up and celebrate."

Joey spun his customer by kicking the metal footrest out of his way. "So the Kennedys are coming to town. You want to burn the barbershop down before they get here? I should complain to city hall."

Chuckling spread along the entire row of off-duty public servants. "It isn't exactly against the law now, is it?" said one of them.

"Maybe I could write some new legislation," said Joey. He kept working and began to hum along with a Tony Bennett song on the table radio. Joey might sing his own song later, moved by the beat of the overhead fan.

The cigar smoker stood, threw his magazine down on a chair to save his place, and went to look at himself in a vacant spot of the panoramic mirror behind the cashier's counter. Maybe the itch on his neck was just the old football coach's instinct telling him something was about to go wrong. That prickling feeling had always been right before.

In the middle of the big man's self-examination, Joey had gone to answer his phone and was taking notes on a pad he kept next to the register. "Yeah, I got it," he said. "On the nose, as usual."

Behind the barber, a row of red leather chairs held the fugitives from city hall, all men in white shirts and inch-wide ties. Off to their right, reflections from the chrome-grilled traffic of Main Street sent glints of morning sun through the shop window.

"What will be your job today, George?"

The big man chewed the end off his cigar and targeted the barber's waste can.

The square metal sides rang as if they had taken a rifle shot. "I get to drive his car, that's all. I'm like Bobby Kennedy's personal tour guide to Cortland, New York."

One of the men in the waiting chairs said, "I didn't know there were many sights to see around here," and the others laughed.

George Clancy, the tallest and most important Democrat in a small town, took his suit coat off a peg by the door and crammed a banded fedora over his balding head. The curled down brim almost hid his tightly-knit eyebrows. "That's confidential information. We don't give out an itinerary, for obvious reasons."

"Name one," someone said from behind a newspaper.

Another man muttered, "The curse, you fool. The Kennedy Curse." With that ringing in his ear, the biggest Democrat leaned into the doorway and hit the open air.

Someone at one of the fraternity houses around the corner was burning leaves. Halloween and drunken college students running down Port Watson Street could not be far behind, and then Election Day. Soon the entire Clancy clan, including some that the big man called "shirt-tail relations and bottom-feeders," would make the rounds of college dormitories and frat houses where they would gather first-time voters and cart them to the polls. Something told the old Democrat he had a chance to follow Robert F. Kennedy to bigger things, and he should drop everything else to make that happen.

In front of a medical arts building, a man dressed in overalls and a wide, drooping felt hat was leaning against a rusted Ford truck with a tarp tied down over the box. He waved at Clancy with one hand as he lit a pipe with the other and drew on it. The two men met as the first puffs of pipe tobacco drifted away.

"How's the big campaign manager? Don't see much of you up at Little York."

"I guess that's cousin Ron Taylor trying to hide under his hat, as usual. You know I can't spend time in little cottage tracts by the lake."

"Sure, and you don't approve of living there either, I guess?" The other man winked at him.

"I approve of living off the land, if that's what you mean. It's just the population density doesn't lend itself to my style of politics."

"Yeah, whatever you just said is fine with me. But my wife still doesn't like what your wife said to her at last year's Christmas party, something about her waist size, so I guess we won't be seeing the two of them over the punch bowl this year."

"Maybe not. But we're still okay, aren't we, Ron? I don't see anything wrong with your waist."

The other man patted his skinny midriff with pride. "Haven't had my lunch yet. I'm waiting for Ron Junior to come back from his weekly counseling session." He nodded to the doctor's office where a wooden plaque announced, "Child Psychology."

"What's he in for? Not shooting the neighbor's cats again?"

"Naw," said Taylor as he puffed away. "Something entirely different, I'd say, like plugging rabbits with a pellet gun. Only these were sort of pet rabbits and the owner in question was sort of related to the county sheriff, if you see my problem."

"You still let Ron Junior go around thinking he's Roy Rogers?"

"Going deer hunting with me in a couple of weeks. Ronnie's 14 now and gotta start earning his keep. These counseling sessions can be right expensive, you know."

"Well, maybe if you didn't encourage him to use the entire countryside as his practice range, he wouldn't get arrested so often and you wouldn't have to take him in to have his head checked."

The senior Taylor grimaced. "Aw, you know the boy's had fainting spells ever since he played on that pee-wee football team you said would build his character. Didn't work out that way, did it? That's why he's got to start hunting now, so he gets it right while I can still teach him. A kid like him might be forced to leave home before he's finished learning to survive."

At that moment the Taylor boy pushed open the door of the doctor's office and propelled his lanky teenage body across the sidewalk. The boy slapped the side of the old Ford's hood with the palm of his hand and it made a booming noise that echoed up and down Main Street, scattering pigeons from the rooftops. "Come on, Dad. We've got logs to split." He yanked the passenger door open, jumped inside, and slammed the door behind him. More pigeons flew.

Clancy leaned close to his cousin's ear and said, "I just hope the rest of us survive your son's survival training."

Crossing the street, Clancy stopped to look in the window of the sporting goods store. He was only there a moment when a flash of chrome slid to the curb behind him. He turned to find a gray Plymouth Belvedere with over-sized tires and a whiplash antenna tied to the trunk. A power window rolled down and the face of a hawkish man with a blond crew-cut appeared where the tinted glass had been.

The blond man pulled some folding money out of his shirt pocket and said, "This hundred dollars says Bobby Kennedy won't make it to Capitol Hill, unless they carry him in. Anybody around here have the guts to bet against me?"

"I would, if I didn't have to feed a houseful of kids and keep my wife in pantyhose." Clancy spit the last of his cigar into the gutter. "You'd think a cop would hide out in a different kind of car than one with a heavy duty suspension package and a police radio on the dash."

The blond man laughed and put his money away. "We need this to pay snitches anyway. The name's Piper. How are you, Clancy?"

"I'm fine except for my memory. Getting old. Where'd we meet before?"

"I worked for Rockefeller when he ran in sixty-two. You were on the losing side. Looks like you might do better this time."

"If you don't muck it up, I will. As I recall, Rocky wasn't too happy with the way you handled things. Something about horse's names appearing on your expense account. I'm guessing you haven't buried that darker side yet. Now you've got me thinking. Were you serious about placing a bet on Bobby Kennedy's life?'"

The blond man laughed. "We try that in every town, just to see if anyone takes us up on it. That could mean there was a certain mindset in the background, some offbeat thinking by loners with too much time on their hands. You know the type."

"Anyone here fit the bill?"

"Not real sure. You could call it a sting, unofficially. A few guys going in and out of that barbershop over there checked their wallets. One guy hauling wood gave us ten bucks to say Kennedy would never make it. We're gonna check on him. I was actually hoping you would be interested, just to give us somebody else to investigate today."

"Right. You think anyone would actually take a shot at Bobby?"

"Not in your town, my man. This is the soul of America. No fanatics allowed."

"That the way you're playing it?"

"We're playing it tight," growled Piper. "I'm right behind Mr. Kennedy with my hand on his belt at every turn. If he wriggles free I've got two other guys to tackle him."

"Okay, just tell me one thing." Clancy paused and arched his eyebrows so they appeared to separate temporarily before returning to their customary uni-brow position. "Why does everyone want me to drive his car? I'm just a guy who happens to be in charge of a campaign this year. I'm not really trained to thwart assassination attempts."

Piper nodded and then tilted his head to one side. "People get hurt sometimes. Look at what happened to the governor of Texas who was just sitting in front of Jack Kennedy. I sympathize. But look at it another way."

Clancy grimaced. "What other way is there to look at it? I might as well think of myself as expendable."

"Think about my job, then. I get to throw myself on his convulsing body at the first sound of gunfire, and I've got to pray to God whoever has the gun doesn't take a second shot. Just think about that. Would you rather have my job, or drive the car?"

When Clancy didn't say anything, Piper backed the Plymouth cruiser out of its slot and yelled, "See you at the Holiday Inn in three hours." He snapped at a cigarette with his lighter and bright embers came out of the car window as it shot away.

Clancy stood in front of the sporting goods store for a while and watched the remnants of burnt tobacco rise and wisp around him until the flakes cooled and descended on his wing-tip shoes. For a moment he had a vision of firewood poking out from under the tarp on Ron Taylor's truck, but he wasn't certain he had really seen it.

It was noon when George Clancy pulled his Oldsmobile into the parking lot of the Cortland Hotel. He got a beer at the bar before going to his usual booth. There he found a man sitting in the far corner where he could not be seen from the rest of the room. He was a large man, fit into a tailored shirt that showed the results of weight training and just a little extra fat. He had a single loop of black hair drooping over a tanned forehead. He seemed content to stare at a glass of beer that had placed on the table, directly in front of the muscled arms he had folded over his chest. Clancy sat down opposite him.

"What took you so long?"

"A lot of politicians at the bar today."

"You gotta do what you gotta do."

Clancy drew on the foam at the top of his glass. "It isn't every day I get to drive the next senator around town. Or get a visit from the captain of detectives."

The policeman shrugged. "Captain Roth is always around. Even if you don't see me, I'm somewhere. It's what you call a physical law of the universe." He pronounced the word as uni-verse, in separate breaths. "So what do you want with an old cop?"

"I've been hearing things about my man, that if he becomes a U.S. Senator, he might run for president next time."

"That bothers who? Republicans? I cry in my beer for them. I often have salty beer when politicians are around. What's it to you, Mister Taller-Than-Thou Democrat?"

Clancy tightened his lips. "Aren't you worried about the motorcade route?"

"No, I'm a detective. Not an event planner. You want to lead a parade down Main Street, talk to the band leader at Cortland High.

He's got experience setting out traffic cones. Now what do you really want?"

Clancy took his first long drink and looked around. There was nobody close by. "I need to know if people are betting on who wins this election."

Roth paused his drinking long enough to chuckle. "You kidding? This is America, where anything is possible, and probably illegal."

"But who would take a bet like that?"

Roth sneered. "It must be you're the only Clancy who doesn't know how to place a bet." The policeman bent over and pretended to whisper. "Why don't you get your hair cut for the big visit. Or is a close shave something you want to avoid?"

Clancy thought out loud. "If you know all the bookies in town, why don't you stop them from doing things like encouraging assassination attempts?" He began rubbing the back of his neck as a precaution against a really illogical answer.

Roth looked sideways but kept talking. "My friend, we arrest the guys on the other end of the phone, not the barber taking the bets. Joey talks to me every day, by the way. Leave him alone. He's mine."

"Would he know if there was anyone betting against Bobby?"

There was a gurgling like laughter and beer being mixed across the table. "He might. I'll ask him. Where will you be in an hour?"

Clancy told him and then finished his beer alone and in silence.

At twelve-thirty the Oldsmobile was in the parking lot of the *Standard*, and Clancy was pushing his way into the glass-walled lobby that angled into Main Street. He cornered a man wearing a half-buttoned vest and slackened tie just as a copy of the day's news landed in a nearby basket labeled 'Mr. Lexton.'

"Today's headline is pretty tame."

"Sorry we can't all be Democrats," was the editor's response. "'RFK On His Way' was the best I could do. You're not worried we won't cover Baby Brother's arrival?"

"Not for a moment. I have some news, though. The FBI has staked out Joey's and tapped his phone. Anybody who called there today is being watched."

"When did putting two bucks on a horse become a federal crime? I do that myself every Thursday."

Lexton got the idea Clancy could use a cigar and drew one out of a drawer in his desk. The two had spent long hours together on the campaign circuit and shared hotel rooms on election night, so they knew each other's vices.

"Watch the ashes. As much as I admire a flaming wastebasket now and then, I've already got a picture for the front page."

"There's some kind of setup," said Clancy, "but a confused one."

"I'm not surprised. I'm confused myself. I thought you were in charge?"

"Yeah. Of a few meet-and-greet sessions later today. There's something bigger coming down, and we'll be hip deep in it tomorrow."

"What do you want from me, the same hip-boots you borrow from my fishing cabin every year?"

"I'm thinking you might try to get subpoenas for any local wire-taps or surveillance and just see what the reaction is. You might not get too far."

"Right. We don't exactly have freedom of information in this country where J. Edgar Hoover is involved, but I could request the documents from the U.S. Attorney's Office in Syracuse. Might take a couple of days to get an answer."

Clancy nodded. "In the meantime, give me a cameraman with close-up lens outside of Joey's as soon as you can."

The double glass doors slammed on his way out.

It was one o'clock and already just two hours before Robert Kennedy was to arrive when the reporter showed up with his camera bag and notepad. He was small but didn't seem to mind that the camera bag was half as big as he was. "My name's Dremler. You Clancy? I think we met somewhere."

"Ever shoot football games?"

"I got it now. You were a coach a couple years back. What happened?"

"Something more important came up."

"If you say so. What's the job then?"

Clancy pointed across the way at Joey's barbershop. "I need an up close shot of the book kept by the register. It has a page where all the barbers look to see who's next. Tell them you're doing a photo story, ask a few questions and pretend to be interested in the answers. When you spot the notebook, snap it and get the hell out of there."

"Okay. Lexton says do what I'm told and keep it hush or I'm back in the mail room. Personally I like strapping bundles, but I get the point. Anything else?"

"I need a blowup of the names on that list in an hour."

Dremler smiled. "The big photographer's out looking for Bobby Kennedy, but I can do this for you." He trotted off, slinging the camera equipment like a soldier toting his weapon behind him.

Left on the sidewalk, Clancy felt the old itch return to the back of his neck and rubbed it violently.

At quarter after one, the skies were gray and Clancy felt clammy in his suit. He walked around the corner to the Youth Center and spotted two teenage boys who were looking in the window, eying the pool table that had recently been donated with the idea of keeping certain young men off the street. For the moment, Clancy was glad these boys were not following the plan.

Clancy called to the boys, a big one and a very much shorter one, and spent a few moments convincing them he was not the local attendance officer. Then he gave them each a pad of paper from the trunk of his car and a few dollar bills from his pocket and told them there would be more money in an hour if they followed the instructions, which he gave in detail.

It was going on 1:30 when Clancy climbed the stairs to the telephone building. He hit the metal door with a thud and felt the air come out of his chest like an old football kicked too hard. He straightened up in time to say hello to the woman at the front desk .

Martha Clancy was an aunt that he knew well enough to ask a favor of when he needed it. He stood and made small talk for just a minute, watching the clock.

"I don't see a lot of you, nephew. It's not like you to come barging in here and spend time trying to be pleasant." She spoke into a stiff black headset that had been clamped down into her fading red curls.

"I wanted to wish you a happy birthday, Martha." Clancy doubted that would get him anywhere, but he was busy thinking about a summer job he had once at this same telephone office, learning how electronic switching systems worked.

"Birthday's not till next week. You don't lie so good, George Clancy. I always told your mother you were duplicitous. So what do you want?"

Clancy decided to check his forehead for sweat.

"About time you took your hat off in front of a lady. I'm busy. I got calls coming in. Don't you have a wife to talk to? How is my niece anyway? Neither one of you ever dial 'O' for operator or I might know these things."

"We're all okay, I guess. I'm a little busy today, of course."

"Too busy for family, as usual. How about my sister's family? Seen them?"

"Saw Ron Taylor and his son downtown a few minutes ago. Why?"

"Just wondering if you could find any Taylors a decent job so they can quit sponging off me, that's all. Young Ron could use a steer in the right direction."

"So I've heard. But I'll have more time to worry about other people once this election is over."

"Be nice if we all live that long," the older woman said.

Clancy stood up. "Mind if I use your bathroom, Martha?"

"First door past the water cooler."

When he was sure she was on a call and not looking, Clancy tried the door to the switch room and it gave way. A whirlwind of electro-mechanical noise made him feel as though he had just stepped into a giant cuckoo clock. He took a moment to get his bearings and then found the traps off to the side, against the wall. He remembered working with them, tracing prank callers and ex-wives who rang phones after midnight and then hung up when someone sleepy answered.

One machine was printing cards and dropping them to a little wire tray below. All Clancy had to do was remember how to read those cards. He rubbed the sweat off his brow again and tried to think.

After five minutes he had written a list of numbers in the memo section of his pocket calendar, and returned the cards to their holder. Then he went out to the water cooler and made some gurgling noises and wiped his forehead again.

Martha Clancy looked up. "Try Frank and Mary's Diner next time."

Clancy said, "You're right, Martha. I need something. I've got to find out who's on the other end of some phone numbers."

"You need a reverse directory. That's not an official phone company service. Not like letting you go pee and then gargle in the water fountain."

"You can't help me? It's kind of important."

She sighed. "I hate this job even more than I hate lying, misbehaving, incontinent nephews who sweat in October, but we're not allowed to give out private information. On the other hand, the Chamber of Commerce has a big cross-reference of addresses and phone numbers, and I think they also have a water cooler and a men's room."

Clancy tried to bend over and kiss her, but she batted him away with one hand while pushing a cord in her switchboard with the other. "Operator, may I help you?"

"Thanks, Martha. I'll get you something for your birthday. If I'm not too busy."

She put a hand over the mouthpiece in front of her. "Kiss that Bobby Kennedy for me. He's a lot cuter than you."

Clancy clutched at his pocket calendar to make sure it was still there, and slid down the stairs.

It was almost 2:00 by the time Clancy talked his way into the Chamber of Commerce offices. It turned out the assistant chamber director was interested in politics, at least as far as learning how close the Kennedy motorcade might be if he leaned out his office window at the right time.

"I'd like to be able to tell my grandchildren I saw a Kennedy once."

"Do you have any grandchildren?" asked Clancy.

"My own children are still in school," the chamber man said while tugging at the stiff collar behind his tie. "I was speaking of potential grandchildren when I'm old and gray."

"No need to rush. My oldest is just fourteen. We call him Georgie because he doesn't like to be called George Clancy the Third, and we're all hoping there won't be a George the Fourth any time soon."

"Oh, I quite understand. Did you find anything in the directory?"

Clancy had made enough small talk for a month. He closed the book he had been searching, and nodded. "Quite." It seemed to him he was making fun of the way the people at the Chamber spoke, but the assistant director didn't seem to notice. The door closed noiselessly on his way out.

Back on Main Street the clock tower said 2:15 and Bobby Kennedy was only forty-five minutes away from entering town. One of the boys Clancy had left outside the sporting goods store was waiting at the curb. Clancy took the writing pads the big boy held out to him and asked, "Only five? Are you sure?"

The boy nodded quickly. "I hit everyone who left after the photo guy, except one really ugly guy I knew was a policeman, but I wrote him down anyway."

"Good work. Any trouble about the names?"

"Not a lick. I told them I was getting up a petition to rename the football field after you, Mr. Clancy, and they all signed up right away."

"It'll never happen, but if they were amused, these signatures might be legit." Clancy held two five dollar bills out the car window. "Don't let me hear you kept more than your share," he said, and drove on.

It was all taking too long. Clancy cursed and took to checking his wristwatch every fifteen seconds as he drove. Sure, he could have skipped some of the chit-chat along the way, but then he wouldn't be totally human. He might not notice when good guys cross the line and become more like bad guys.

"About time you showed up," Lexton called out across the newsroom. "I've got things to do besides figure out who's getting a haircut today. And why is that important, anyway?"

Clancy took out his notes and laid them side-by-side with the blowups the photographer had made from the barbershop. He held the list of names the tall boy and the short boy had added by watching the barbershop while he was gone.

Lexton was chewing on an unlit cigar. He was good at chewing and not mangling. He could point the cigar in four different directions and then start all over again without dripping any of the tobacco. Clancy thought Lexton was better at this cigar-chewing act than any of the make-believe newspapermen you would see in the movies or on TV.

Clancy pointed to his list. "You set a trap by dialing your own number after a prank call. A card is punched with your phone number on it and dropped right on top of the last caller's card."

"You're amazing, Clancy. And I suppose you told the FBI you were tapping into their tap, so it's all legal and what-not?"

Clancy grinned. "You know what a sting is?"

Lexton twiddled his cigar. "That's when you bait a hook and hope some critter comes along and bites it. We've been fishing together, so I know that. What's on the other lists?"

"Guys who actually got their hair cut today."

"So the rest must be…"

"People who didn't want haircuts, of course."

The receptionist interrupted their thoughts. "Call for you gentlemen." Lexton grabbed a nearby extension and punched it up. A second later he was handing the receiver to Clancy. The receptionist added, "Sounds like a policeman."

Clancy took it and listened for a while and then handed the phone back to Lexton. "Eleven o'clock this morning, give or take ten minutes. That's when Joey told the police he took a bet on Kennedy's life. Joey gave the city police a name for the guy who started it all, but it turned out to be phony. Only a few FBI men would know who really made that call, because they made it, and they're sitting in a ballroom at the Holiday Inn, not at city hall, so it's you and me."

"Somebody will need to go to church for a year to make up for all this."

"Not me, but the guys who concocted this scheme will need a lot of forgiveness."

Lexton was frowning at Clancy's list. "Hold on to your fedora and check this out. Somebody named Taylor called at 12:32. Don't you have a cousin named Taylor?"

Clancy swore. He had been driving and talking so much he hadn't paid much attention to the names he had written down while talking at the Chamber of Commerce. The Taylors lived up near Little York Lake, between two roads that came down from Syracuse. He pushed Lexton aside and grabbed the editor's phone. "Do you mind?"

Little York was a maze of twisting roads that led down to a green lake between the Interstate and the county highway. The Oldsmobile's carburetor had a thorough cleaning by the time Clancy pulled up to the split-rail fence and ran down to one of the boat docks. He had the motor on Lexton's boat charging out into the lake with five minutes to go.

As Clancy steered, he felt tiny hairs on his neck prickling their way up. He tugged at his collar and loosened it, but only enough to arch his neck and see around the next bend. He thought he saw cars moving toward the dock behind him, but didn't look back.

The way Little York flowed was to divide itself into two parts, one where people camped out and had picnics, and another on the other side of the highway where no one but teenagers went when they wanted to be alone. Between the two halves of the lake, a small channel ran alongside the highway and turned under a bridge that was so low Clancy had to duck his head to get through. He went to the far end, where the lake ran up against the highway, and coasted Lexton's boat to the shore. The sound of passing trucks overpowered any sloshing of tiny waves against the wooden hull.

There is an art to walking so no one hears you, an art practiced by big men, older men, men dressed in suit coats and skinny ties, men afraid of what they might find. This lake was where he had come in the days of his youth, to get away from adults and be sure that no one would bother him. He had spent many hours here, floating in a boat, or lying in the soft grass that overlooked the highway from a little rise at the water's end.

It was near the top of the rise, at the farthest end of the lake, hidden by the soft grass, that he found 14-year-old Ron Taylor's thin frame lying prone amid the yellow and orange colors of the autumn ground, collapsed over his father's hunting rifle that still pointed toward a row of cars heading into town.

Clancy checked his watch just once as he picked his way forward. It was 2:59 and the Kennedy motorcade was overdue, but not by much. Clancy eased a short breath out of his lungs and reached down to withdraw the rifle without a word.

The Taylor boy rolled over groggily. He had some mud on his face from time spent unconscious on the damp ground. Sun winked in the boy's eyes and he had to raise a hand to shade himself and see the man standing over him. "Uncle George? I must of had one of my seizures and passed out. I feel all jittery."

Clancy had turned around already. "Come with me," was all he said. He got in Lexton's boat and went back to the dock trusting that Ron Junior would be behind him, in some other boat he hadn't seen but knew was there.

At the base of the pavilion, Lexton was waiting for him along with Roth, whose bronzed, folded arms made him larger than life, as if he had been placed there by the parks commission. Lexton shifted position as he toyed with an old camera he had brought along, probably the one he used to take pictures of fish.

As Clancy tied up the boat, he heard oars kicking up the water behind him and Ron Junior was there at his side. "Uncle, how did you find me?"

"Playing a hunch is all. Don't you ever do that?"

"My dad says I'm not old enough to gamble, but if I stay out of trouble, he'll show me how it works someday." The boy looked back at the rifle in Lexton's boat, wondering if he should take it. "I might not ever want to learn now."

There was a gravel hill between Clancy and the other men. He had a few seconds to talk without being heard. "What were you doing, exactly?"

The boy shook a little. "I was just going to make some noise and hope they turned around. I wasn't shooting at anybody. You know the bet Dad made?"

Clancy nodded. "That Bobby Kennedy wouldn't make it to Cortland. I guess you figured your Dad needed money pretty bad. You can blame me for part of that. I haven't been paying attention to things like I should lately." He looked over at the big highway in time to see three Cadillacs going by, with a Lincoln or two trailing behind.

"Who's going to know I was here?"

Clancy nodded toward the two men at the top of the gravel path. "These men. One has a camera and another has a set of handcuffs. They don't know who you are, but I got to tell them."

Ron Junior looked back at the rifle in the boat again and Clancy said, "I'll take care of that, too."

A crowd had gathered at the Holiday Inn, and a speech was being made. Clancy found the FBI man with his back against the rear wall of the ballroom.

"You're late," said Piper under his breath.

Clancy got up close to Piper's ear and whispered, "I won't tell anybody if you don't."

Piper looked at him sideways. "About where you been? Come to think of it, where have you been?"

"Somewhere I haven't been in years, chasing down a slightly deranged kid who overheard his father making a bet on a certain politician's life."

Piper curled his lips and cocked his head toward Clancy. "You know what a government operation is? You want to get in the way of that?"

Clancy poked Piper with a stiff finger and made him jump just a bit. "I already have. I found out about it and squashed it. If you want to say I'm out of line, go and try. I'm sure Bobby would love to hear about what you did."

Piper looked up at nothing in particular. "Don't you know what the Bureau and the Secret Service do? We keeps secrets. Kennedy doesn't run Justice anymore. He doesn't know what they're doing or what I'm doing. He can just be thankful we're here. Am I right?"

Clancy moved away, slowly. The speaker at the podium was about to introduce the next senator from the great state of New York. The crowd was buzzing and Clancy thought he could shout back at the FBI man now and nobody would hear him, or believe him if they did.

"I'm not so sure what Bobby's people will think about this. But

I'll try to explain it so they don't hang the both of us. You're creative, Piper, I like that. Only, you ran a play that didn't work and now your own team is nervous about you. Frankly, I'd punt."

Piper turned to the wall and buried his face in the deep curtains he found there. The fabric smelled of small town smoke and traveling salesmen, three-piece bands and masters of ceremonies in rented suits. He muttered just loud enough for someone next to him to hear, "Clancy, you're a piece of work."

After the parading and the band playing and the handshaking, Clancy went down to the jail and sat with young Taylor in an interview room. Roth came in and did his famous folded-arms act. The police captain cleared his throat and said, "I told the DA what I knew and he said to throw the book at this kid, whether he's one of your relatives or not and whether he's got mental disabilities or not. So he's being charged with three weapons violations and trespassing on a state right-of-way and hunting out of season. That's several hundred dollars worth of fines, or he spends time in some government housing. And there's got to be a psychologist in here in a few minutes."

Ron Junior was breathing a little fast and reaching for a cup of water that Roth had brought for him. "What does that all mean?"

Roth said, "It means the DA is running for office this fall, like a lot of people we seem to know, and none of them want a disadvantaged youngster taking the fall for what stupid adults do, and you can quote me on that. My boss and his boss and everybody else's boss agree that setting up a sting is tricky business and has got to be done right. This was a botch job by some people who should know better and have been invited to leave town as nicely as we can."

Clancy laughed softly. "That first part was my work. I invited them to leave. The nice part was somebody else."

Roth nodded. "That would have been the mayor, our congressman, and a few people from the governor's office who just happened to be in town."

Ron Junior blinked. "So what happens to me?"

Clancy slapped him on the back. "You sit here and wait for me to explain this to your parents and a certain newspaperman I know. Meanwhile you get a meal courtesy of the city, and maybe a stiffly padded bed while I try to find somebody who has enough money to pay your fines and spring you. That should take only a couple of days."

"Days?"

"Don't worry," said Clancy as he rose to go. "I've got a long list of big-hearted Cortland citizens I can call. I'm bound to find someone in this tough little corner of the world who won't hang the Kennedy curse on your skinny neck."

FATHERS, SONS, GHOSTS, GUNS

by Gary Cahill

"Pride goeth before destruction,
and a haughty spirit before a fall..."
Proverbs 16:18 -- Webster's Bible Translation

"You'll catch your death..."
-- Everybody's Mom

Happy holidays. And an extended celebration it was for Win Racklin, *El Jefe*, as he called himself, of the venerable Racklin Oil Works, who'd added to the calendar a date of remembrance leading up to Thanksgiving. Some years, WinDay and T-Day coincided on the fourth November Thursday, but usually Win's new entry fell a few days ahead to harken and herald the oncoming traditional season, and he often flew east out of Dallas/Fort Worth to play king of the world, spread around some ill will; to engage and abuse and put a spurred boot to some of the little people who'd made it possible and been left behind.

With Win in back, Errol pulled away from the field of Bombardier Lears and Gulfstream 5s and 6s at Teterboro and tooled the big car through the maze of Jersey roads, 46 to 95 to 495 headed right toward New York. Win would have Errol turn off before hitting the city, first sightseeing and contemplating the sweep of a violent history along the Hudson County coast, then making his courtesy calls.

The view from the Weehawken cliffs played it out. Now developed and condoed over, the old freight piers and railroad yards still peeked through, where the Irish and Italian mobs ran the shipping, the Teamsters and Hoffa ran the trucking, and liaisoning with the big New York families was up to Tony Pro, lording over Local 560 in neighboring Union City, his limo a gray and black shark, every morning cruising past the locals, who all knew how hungry a predator it could be. This was Havana North back then, where so many Cuban expats wound up after Castro took over, and never stopped lusting to return to their native Caribbean cradle. When all you have and know is gone, and each new day, dawn after dawn, relumes a deadend disheartening vista of factory smoke, poison plumes of chemical plant spew and diesel showers settling over grime crusted snow, who could blame them? Or, comes a time, who wouldn't probe for the soft spot, deep in the homesick gut, and *use* them? And for having their fingers on that pulse, kudos and thanks flowed from Win, and all the rest, to his sainted Daddy and Granddaddy, the creators of The Curse, and the guarantors of their family's blessed legacy.

Win would pay respects to 560, so overtly corrupt it was the first union local in the country's history to be forcibly taken over by the federal government, and have Errol drive by the old headquarters on the way to Cuba on the Coast, Fine Hand-Crafted Cigars.

◊ ◊ ◊ ◊ ◊

"Proprietor, Osvaldo Veciana. Look, right there on the glass, oh God, the guy's name, Errol, I told you. I nailed it, on both ends, I got it coming and going. Did my homework finding this guy. Had to be my choice."

Errol had trouble seeing the front window because he had trouble getting out of the car. He was big—real big; none of it flab.

Errol also had trouble understanding what Win would be doing tonight and tomorrow, this meat-headed, mean-spirited merry making. Why can't he be satisfied, sated, allayed with victory? Maintain some sense, show some grace? All of it so long ago, and *none* of it *his* doing. The other players, including the family under the mantle of the laughingly labeled 'curse', lived with defeat.

Well, not all of 'em.

Ah, it was not for him to say, and he anyway didn't talk much. Errol was a hired pair of hands—how the Racklins did things—and with those hands did what needed to be done. Win doled out the browbeating; Errol, the other kind. Let the unmanning begin.

The Stars and Stripes, a gilded fringe version, flipping through an evening breeze in a flag stand on the sidewalk, the door centered on a double window storefront, and it was straight back past the displays to the owner's buffed dark wood desk.

Win did not wait to stir it up. "So, Mr. Oswald, does 'Cuban cigars' only mean rolled by Cubish *señores* such as yourself from inferior tobacco, or can I infer you offer the real thing?"

"The 'real thing' as you call it has been illegal here for a long time. And my name is, properly in the United States, Mr. Veciana." Veciana felt no need to allow any sardonic twinkle in his eye. He had that fisherman's hard build and patinaed skin, a beautiful pro barber's scissor cut, nicely grown out, all swept back salt and pepper, an older man than he looked.

"Yeah, that's the shame of it, eh, Ozzie? Castro runs you out, and believe me, the stogie smokers here were just outraged, totally on your side, and you all get stuck here since forever. Never got back home, did you? No matter how much you paid, what you bombed, whoever's cars you blew up, you couldn't shoot your way back, couldn't kill enough, whatever you thought it took. Just nobody gave a loose, watery shit about you."

The vile Spanish swearing in Veciana's mind turned his face an olive red.

"Do I know yo…just who the fuck are you?" Veciana got lighter in his leather and lacquer chair, snaking a hand under the desk drawer. Win didn't notice, but it wouldn't matter, because the move got Errol's attention.

"Me? Oh, you don't want my name. You'll never get it out of your head after this. Soon you'll wish you didn't know me at all…" and the desk toppled straight back onto Veciana with a diving Errol splayed on top. The furniture was ripped to the side and Errol snarled and spat, a coyote on a wounded limping herd lagger, and his arms pistoned into Veciana's head and throat and ribs.

Errol stood and breathed wide, then knifed down at the waist to right-left snap-slap him two fat ones on the temples, big, loud, whack 'n' whack, and walked away with the gun from the desk drawer.

"I can get fuckin' cigars from Canada, Mexico, almost anywhere, no trouble, we know that. Done it a million times. I'm here to mark territory. To remind you. And the rest."

Win saw one eye moving in Veciana's head, knew he was getting through, then bent over and whispered the names of his beloved Lone Star hometown, and his Daddy, and an autumn date from decades ago. The Cuban's eye lit up and burned like blue coal.

"I'm going to get them from you, and I'm going to pay whatever it takes, I don't give a shit, whatever you say, but you're going to do it for the money. *For the money.* The only reason you should ever do anything. And learn that lesson. I found you. I chose *you*. Your last name—it was an *hombre* named Veciana who founded Alpha 66 way back when, and those bastards would have blown up half the world to get back home to Havana. He was a close relative, perhaps? As if your first name wasn't regal enough in all this. I mean, really, *Oswald*, can you believe it? Should add a book for him in the Bible."

The martyr, Win had often thought of him. More like the sacrificial lamb.

"You listen to me, when they all say it's not about the money, it is. And if through some miracle it's *really not* about the money, it should be. It puts limits on all the lying, 'cause everyone knows where they stand. How the world turns, right, there, Ozzie? We'll be in touch. I'll speak to you."

Osvaldo Veciana, throat crushed closed, seething, tried to swear out loud; he wouldn't be speaking to anyone for quite a while.

"Errol," who was back behind the wheel and rolling along the last soft Lincoln Tunnel curve into New York, "let's skip through Manhattan, head over the Brooklyn Bridge to the Borough of Kings, visit the Genoveses."

The old place, the real place where it happened, with all the checkered tablecloths and gaslight fixtures, was gone, closed up after a hundred years of red sauce and sit-downs, and long rides to last rites. Few knew that Don Vito himself, and the family, had been heavy investors in the Texas energy industry way back to the 1950s, and so were all too glad to oblige a few years later with use of the back room when some well-oiled, high-powered, untraceable "machinery" needed to be carefully wrapped, cloth bagged, packed into long wooden crates, driven to Baltimore to divert any prying eyes, and flown on out to Fort Worth, en route to being put to use in Dallas.

With time having claimed a century of Mauro's Venice Ristorante, Win found Sal's, a classic wiseguy pizzeria, so mob movie clichéd in every way you couldn't tell if art imitated life or the other way around. Except for the food, no fakery there, which was totally aces, making it all the more fun for Win to rear up and back and kick like the wild stallion he dreamed he was and really bust some "meatballs", he loved to say to the boys back home. Win ran down a magical seafood salad as basement level cat food, the excellent eggplant a step up from barnyard pen slop, and on and on—jes' drawlin', and moanin', all 'bout how bad it all wuz. "*Boy*, another drink, boy." And then.

"Hey, y'all, this pizza," which was nearly perfect in every way, "you know, it's a little dark around the edges, wouldn't you say? Maybe even burnt." Didn't know how much he sounded like one of those touchy-fluffy blonde families from the 'burbs.

There's a get away with it guy and a wrong guy to say this to at Sal's. Pietro, universally known as Rock, had lived too long, and through too much, and was the wrong guy. No little pizza wheel; he cut slices with a mezzaluna or, tonight, a chef's knife. Wielded more like a broadsword every second. He spoke, in perfect Brooklyn Pizzaioli.

"Yeah, it's crispy around the edges. And blood red right through the middle, you cracker cowboy son of a bitch." Rock caught Errol's eye and waited, remembering Win's last visit, and all the fun they'd had with the insurance agents afterward. Errol was more than ready, but Win made no move. So Rock, ever a gracious host, and all things considered, decided to let them eat while he tripled the bill, providing a lyrical "cracker", "cowboy", "son of a bitch" serenade as he walked away to clean up the kitchen. Pot banging. Loudly. Even for him.

Out the door at Sal's, the 300% and then some tip having reduced a confused and defeated Rock to apoplectic stammering, an ever more booze-happy Win was already plotting his next bulldozing.

"First thing tomorrow," urrpping and snorting, "hey, we're in fuckin' New York City, how about we join our Hebrewish brothers for those bagels and salmon and cream cheese, but then ask for that chicken fat schmaltz shit and pour it all over everything, oh, I'd make that a scene, I'd love that."

Errol was confused.

"Jews? With you guys? Jews were in on this deal?" Errol was no academic. He'd always believed with the *chosen people* and those hymn-humming, old-wooden-cross-burning broncobusters, it was never *those* twain to meet, whether in or out of their Christian uniforms —the dress-white sheets, and hoods, and sidearms.

Win's mood downshifted, shook his head, disappointed with Errol's ignorance of history.

"The mob money man, the little rabbi from Florida, the real king of 'em all, who just *ruled* all those Mr. Mario Mafios, *he* wanted in, and he much more than just *chipped* in, didn't he? And how about the guy who shoots a murder suspect in front of a hundred cops, shuts him up for good, takes the fall? Would *that* be 'in on this' enough for ya? Oh, no, no Jews. God, no."

A red light allowed Errol to stare at the floor, properly chastened. But Win knew what Errol meant. There'd been a couple garden-weed variety hebes that Granddaddy'd added to the "city business council" back home in the early '60s for appearance's sake, but the Star of David did not help light the way for the eyes of Texas. At all. Let's say they would remain disenfranchised in serious matters of local commerce and politics.

The car was moving over the East River back into Manhattan, and Win was really feeling the drink. "Look at that. The skyscrapers. All lit up, like big, pulsing dicks, burning all night, going all night long. And that's all they want, all these guys, that's why they do everything. Sex, ass-kicking, revenge. All insults answered double. Triple. All that macho pride bullshit."

"Good thing you're above all that, sir."

"Shut up, Errol."

Win drooled and spit on his shirt, kept going. "It's why, it's how we…could *utilize* them all, how Daddy and Granddaddy and the rest of them worked it. Nobody else got what they wanted from what we all did. Not these Cubans, not these Italian mob guys, not the fuckin' micks in with them in the unions. That's another *real* 'curse' in all this, these guys are all cursed forever, not that mystical romantic mumbo-jumbo-headed bullshit…"

And Win could have sucked a whole pile of bullshit through his teeth with that brand new grin stretched across his red and white face. Last time this had been big fun. He'd push a little harder this time.

"Hey, maybe let's hit that midtown Irish bar for breakfast, find some mickey pricks gettin' sloppy early and trash their American Royal Family."

Errol knew the score.

"You mean the Bushes?"

They laughed so, so hard.

And then Win, well, he loved hearing it as much as saying it.

"Nah, the dead and gone *begorah* slingin' 'Johnny we hardly knew ye' Royal Family."

◊ ◊ ◊ ◊ ◊

Sun up, flaring through the knighted towers of Manhattan, their shadows cast and falling west, shading Hell's Kitchen, as always. In a big old joint on the corner, open early and very late, Win and Errol were digging into what looked like buckets of the Traditional Irish Breakfast, that sausage links and patties with fat-mashed filled stuffing over bacon and black blood pudding gravy coated heart-stopper. Morning looked to have broken the backs of the two regulars down the bar; the hewn Italianate muscle, and the frayed around the edges Amer-Irish whitey Racklin had enraged with indecorous conversation last time he was in town. Bookie and loan shark leg-breakers, Win recalled. Looked not to have slept in two days, minimum. And looked soft, at least today. These two would be engaging an Alternative Irish Breakfast; Guinness and Jameson, neat.

Muscles said "Guinnie Jamie," and stalled, out of gas.

Frayed Edges found the language. "Guinnie Jamie. Please. Thanks, Stella. Thank you." He stopped talking, shut down the cruise control, slumping, and double shots appeared while Stella began the draught pulls and chirped, "Shot o' clear with a black beer, clean shot with a black spot." Looking back, smiling over her shoulder. She hoped her birdy voice annoyed them, the way you poke friends when they're down, at least around here. With a sharp stick if one's handy.

Win chimed in, more to the point.

"Guinea, you said? So which part o' that set-up's the Eye-talian? Must be the foaming-at-the-mouth on that beer glass. Nah, that's all you mad-dog Irish, too. Sheeeit."

Frayed Edges, standing quickly, slope shouldered, slack hair falling on either side of a wide green-eyed stare, Muscles up and looking like he could splinter the place, other milling friends of the house now attracted to the flame. Errol was right there, always, blocking for Win, but maybe not ready for all this.

"G, G, take it easy, please," Stella called to Frayed Edges. "Willy, please." Muscles turned to her, turned back. "Breakfast service's over; hope you enjoyed your stay."

"I know you," said G. "Last year. Some shit about Daddy and Granddaddy. Yip-yapping your fucking head off."

"Head off." Win's memory conjured wounds from a November day, long ago. "That's funny."

Win waited.

G got it. "Oh, that's right. Texas. Dallas. Fuck you." And Willy grabbed him to keep G from going on past his *"See you out west one day, hey, boys?"* Will knew the big quiet guy was trouble. And the tavern's two resident sleepyheads needed a nap.

Win and Errol paid and left. Threw in their wake some *"ceegars"* hand-rolled by the sons of Cuban Freedom Fighters, right over there in New Jersey." Dropped a tip bigger than what Stella would make all day and tomorrow; dropped it, with a "here ya go, darlin'" flourish, on the barroom floor, because Win knew it was way too much to pass up. But he didn't know Stella.

"What the hell," and Willy let G go, "is wrong with you? You know all this. Shit, you're the one told *me* about the guns out of Brooklyn and the heroin thing from France to New Orleans to here, and Havana and Hoffa and all of it together."

G grinned. "Yeah, you said to me, 'You know about that, huh?' and you told me how some old guy at a card game downtown with your...*associates*...spilled it all, years ago, and you thought it was a fairy tale."

Willy grinned back. "I love it. 'Some old guy'. How about 'venerated elder in a position to know'? Oh, and sorry, I left out the cowboys and their oil."

"Yes. You did. With those fake-ass bullridin' rodeo clowns it's *always* nothing but the money, buying other hands for dirty work, and the bastards throw more and more money at a button until it piles up heavy and the button gets pushed," and G's feet were nearly leaving the floor. "But, one day, my man, me and you and that guy—"

"And, on that day, I will remind you the Lord says 'vengeance is mine'."

"And, Padre Guillermo, I will then remind *you* how we are all made in His image, and ought act accordingly. Preferably Old Testament accordingly. They have bunker busters back then? A pillar of fire will do."

No one else had moved, toward Win's cash or anywhere else; waiting for the all-clear. And certainly not Stella. Because it was only money, and because she felt, in her heart of hearts, it came from a piece of dripping pigshit with a wallet. So the two of them picked it up, the whole lot of it, slid around the bar to stuff it into the tip cups, and sat back down to continue drinking breakfast, and talk about something else. They'd save the cigars for later, outside.

"G, know what?" Stella, back to poking her friend, looking for that pointy stick, working hard to move on before her consuming anger over Racklin's act turned to tears of rage. "The guy told me a pretty funny joke. Come on, I'm just sayin'. It was...got it, here it is. You know, if donkeys were rabbits—"

"Is this going somewhere, or am I just going to get angry?"

"Angry? At me?" Flapping the lashes.

She was right. Not in a million years.

◊ ◊ ◊ ◊ ◊

Win's festive sojourn was over for this year. In this God-blessed America you're only truly cursed if you don't finish first, and he loved playing the screaming eagle U.S. Steel-taloned raptor, lighting on the chicken coop, preying on all these dumb cluckers, maintaining the pecking order. But he needed to get back home, and explain the facts of life, and business, and history, and visit the spoils of winning on the prince, the heir apparent, his son, Victor. This is when they'd establish sharing the corporate titles, the paint on the glass office doors, the imprints on the desk top name plates, the everywhere African mahogany, and the stonecutting on the outside of the buildings; monuments, really, to a monumental past. Sharing the open secrets.

Winfield Adams Racklin/Victor Corson Racklin, and so on and so forth.

◊ ◊ ◊ ◊ ◊

Victor was appalled, having none of it, thought he should make a break for the street and call the cops. Who were these people?

He was not them.

For one thing, he'd spent too much time, certainly too much to suit his father, working with Habitat for Humanity along the nature-scarred and, of all things, oil-poisoned Gulf Coast. And for another, not taken aside and informed until now, he was over-bowled with Daddy's lecture on the family backstory. He wasn't a rube about big boys and business and the ugly nature of deep caring about uncountable riches, but this was unfathomable.

It'd started like this.

"Thank Christ you're back from that pointless hellhole on the Gulf and ready to get—"

"Please, Daddy, not again. Jesus, Katrina and BP and every other goddamned thing down there's not enough? You know why I do it. All my money's from nothing, and…" *oops*, he tried to cover the gaffe, "well, sorry, it's not from *nothing, please*, I know the history."

"You know the written history, the half of it, the agreeable fiction.

A true life myth, if there is such a thing, an epic, is what it really is, about men who were titans, bigger and gutsier and goddamn *righter* than other men. The men who blessed us." Third bourbon already, up and straight down, leaving the branch water-back untouched. Win's hands now in front of him and conducting an invisible amen chorus as he launched into it.

"I named you Victor, and your mother, bless her, just went along, because I knew you'd already won the game, favored before you were even thought of. Son, it went like this. Your granddaddy and great granddaddy and their friends were working oil in east Texas, wildcattin', when it all hit in the '30s. They couldn't know it then, but they went to bat for all of us when they took on the big companies, stood up and didn't sell out to the corporates, gambling on what they were sittin' on. Found the biggest oil pools of all time, drilled and drilled, did it all, and the Feds take the property, by force."

Smack, and Win nearly busted his whiskey tumbler all over his desk. Victor, still seated, was at full attention. Seemed like a good time to start sipping at his drink. He gulped instead.

"Guns and soldiers and hell almighty. It was the goddamn eastern bankers' and Wall Street's fuckin' Great Depression, not ours." Like reading today's paper, Victor thought. Some things *never* change.

"Forcin' us to bail out the whole country and Roosevelt and all that shit, 'cause we all weren't pumping *enough*, of *our own oil*, and wanted us to *give* it away. The United States of America against the United State of Texas. Jesus, you *hold* the product back, *control* production, it drives up *demand*, it's simple, and our price goes *up*. That's how it's *supposed* to work."

The fourth tumbler got his words out faster, blithesome, like holy-rolling. Doctrinaire.

"They actually sent Federal troops to take over our land and then force oil out of the ground and screw with our rightful reward. Franklin Roosevelt," sneering and spitting it out. "Son, so I hear, they all threw a cocktail party celebration in '45 when he died." Win had flashed on saying FDR "kicked the bucket", just to be cruel, but he pulled the cripple joke, and saved a private laugh for later. "Not that Truman taking over was any better. Was not one of us, that shit heel hayseed." Win took a long pull on number five. Getting to it.

"So," Victor said, setting it straight, "at the height of the Great Depression, they conspire to hold nearly all the oil in the country back? Up 'til the Feds stepped in? What the fuck, Dad? They were *proud*...you're *proud* of this, even *now*?"

Victor, having done pretty much nothing in his life but build houses to, in all fairness, impress chicks, right then felt superior to those who'd put him in the big comfy chair. A little rise of self-righteousness made him unaware of his pissing on Mount Olympus, not understanding the gods who...*manipulated* things, like luck, failure, death, success. And Victor didn't see his father, under the collar, break into a big sweaty panic.

"And then we...*they* got ready for the war, son, World War II," the words wet and loose. "Just so good for us. Oil, uranium mines, minerals, guns, all that hardware and machinery, and aircraft, just tons of aircraft, all around Dallas. Son, every kind of stuff to make things go 'boom', and you start hoping for more wars to, I don't know, *supply*. Maybe just a great big forever war."

"Like now?" Victor thought about standing, but thought better of it when his left knee didn't respond. *How dry I was*, he snorted to himself. *Next I'll be drooling.*

Win sniggered out every derisive laugh sound he had, all at once. "Oh, *please*, get it *together*, Mister Racklin Junior," and he hacked out a garbled tribal whoop. "*Whooo*, never thought I'd say it, but thank God for Communists. Granddaddy and them all truly hated all that Socialist shit, like the scum we have now. Like the poor, they're always with us, right? But hats off to those reds. Them being around for the Cold War kept it all going on for us. And Vietnam was like your biggest birthday present ever. Except that fuckin' Kennedy figured it out."

Win the thespian grabbed the sides of his head to hold in the faux rage, and the too real liquor. "He thought money coming our way could be spread around at home to every fuckin' minority or piece of shit group that would vote for him. The way they told me, Daddy and Granddaddy said he was a traitor bastard 'cause he wouldn't pull the trigger on Russia or Cuba, either take 'em over or wipe 'em away. A Commie appeaser."

Win, riding the whiskey, flashed on an inebriate's clarity. "I don't know if you could really blame him. Probably saved the world, I guess for sure, with those nuts of generals advising the Joint Chiefs. They just couldn't wait to nuke 'em all with planes and bombs and missiles. Jack wasn't any idiot, just on the wrong side of history, in the end. But what our family and friends *really* cared about was the money. The free money."

"Daddy, where the hell is this going? What's free money? You make it sound like they *invented* money in the east Texas fields."

Win looked at the floor, braced himself. A lot of rehearsal led to this theater piece. And the audience was much larger than Victor knew.

"We'd…well, they…put it on the line. Like the old Wild West stories, ranchers holding off homesteaders and the railroad. No law, no cops, no judges, just big strapped-in balls and loaded guns, and down in the ground half the whole world's supply of totally golden black oil. And Victor," Win close to staggering in his speech, already afraid, "son, to get to the reason why, Kennedy said he was going after the giant upfront tax break the oil boys enjoyed. Had for decades."

"How much?"

"Twenty seven and a half."

"*Percent?*"

"Percent."

"Off the top?"

"Off the top."

"Christ."

"Called it too big a giveaway to one business. And then he'd start taxing us *overseas*, for God's sakes. Called it unfair *not* to, 's what the President said. Hundreds of millions of *1963 dollars* we're talking here," was what Win said. "Tried to force Big Steel to, Jesus almighty Christ, roll back a price hike, and they caved to get a shitty goddamn labor deal—the Feds' fingers just everywhere, price-fixing, everything. But Lord a' mighty, Daddy and Granddaddy saw what was coming next."

Yes, what was next.

"Kennedy's father, Joe, the" rolled his eyes "*alleged* Prohibition rumrunner, was in with the old big city outfits up to his nostrils.

So was the election, they say, and Jack's crazy brother Bobby starts a crusade, tryin' to send them all off to fuckin' jail. And they're outraged—Miami, Chicago, New Orleans really big-time—very hard men who helped build the family power and fortune, and helped put them into the White House. So the boys put them in the crosshairs. Or so the story goes, of course."

Win took a breath. And another belt from his glass, thinking one thing he shared with Joe Kennedy was an appreciation of the 'water of life', as they called it on the auld emerald sod across the Atlantic.

Victor hadn't moved, other than tugging at his own whiskey. He was looped. But one too many "Kennedy"s tipped him to where this was going. He didn't buy it; didn't want to.

"Dad, stop." Dad wouldn't stop. This was all he'd ever really had to hang onto. It was plenty.

"Jack's popularity was crazy, over 60 percent and going up, no Republican would even be a challenge to him, no way he wouldn't be re-elected, and an in-the-pocket ol' boy Texas oil man" and God, Win loved this part of the tale, "was the sitting Vice-President, next in line to be hailed if something *untoward* were to happen to the chief. Which it did."

"Oh, come on, Daddy. When I'm a kid, you tell me about Christmas and the North Pole, and now I'm older and it's believe in the Grassy Knoll?"

"Yes, Victor. It's true. There is a Santa Claus."

"So you, I mean, Granddaddy and Great-Granddaddy killed the President of the *United States* just for…more money?" Victor, getting a little shaky, floating, like his head was unfastened.

A solid certain future was fading from Win's view. There are winners. And losers. Curses, and victims.

"It might as well have been all the money in the world. There were three of 'em, lined up to be kings, son. Jack, Bobby, and the third brother Ted was already a senator. Victor, everybody with any juice wanted that bastard taken out. And it's talk, talk, talk. Nothing happens until money changes hands, and we had plenty of that. So all over the place, word's out it could really happen, and everybody wants in; like I said, New Orleans, Chicago, Miami, then New York, New Jersey. Oh, New Orleans and Dallas, really big. The Cuban exiles, the mobbed-up Teamsters union, even the hard-ass military and those crazy spooky spy guys, and all them white boys laying for Martin Luther King. *Now*, of course, they all have their own myths. How many men, and women for that matter, have rambled around the country, around the world, got loaded drunk and high and laid spilling stories about the day they pulled a trigger and changed history? Well, somebody's telling the truth. And money's what talks."

Win raised his glass toward his son. Victor didn't care to return the salute, maybe couldn't if he wanted to. His arms were floppy, his eyes hanging.

"But these other...*people* were all in it for the wrong reasons. Who got what they wanted? Is Fidel gone, or Raul? Are the mob resorts and casinos banging all night long in Havana? No, no, and no. There's still a Commie country ninety miles from Florida, and the Mafia's been cut to ribbons from what they once were. That's the 'curse', too, Victor. The curse is on all of *them*. We were the cash daddies, and now they pay for what we did, like it says in the Good Book. But I don't think the Bible ever considered that the fathers would live on past all that mortal sinning, and pass the payment down."

Win laughed about it all, again, so hard.

"You're *my* father, Dad. What about my curse? What's passed down to me? Living with it?" Win was taken aback by "living"; didn't show it.

Two big drinks knocked down, and Victor was flattened. One had been waiting for him, with the double-dose of GHB and Rohypnol, to quell his attitude if things went wrong. With audio bugs all over the office, a good number of ears belonging to very serious people were assessing the flow and dynamic of this not so private father/son conversation. They were listening for the voice of a new team player.

They were disappointed.

"Daddy, I can't, I can't. This is horrible. Who are you people? This is not like some..." and he gave up.

"Sure, I know, not like every banana up your ass republic in the world where there was a *coup* every week. It's what they all say, first time anyone gets it. The real story."

Win would finish the spiel, but he knew the other ears could not be happy with what they were hearing. And there was commitment to a course of action.

"Come on, it was organized, Vic. It took contracting for experts, not a bunch of crazy goombah henchmen or wide-eyed anti-Castro maniacs or racist super-patriot Minutemen. No Kool-Aid drinkers; no *tea* sippers, if you know what I mean. You do hire some of them, use them for recon and decoy and busywork, and they love you forever, like lapdogs. Then you put can't-miss pros in the buildings and on the ground. And, yes, behind the fence on the little grass hill."

Win had been told four shooters. Took a look at the street map, the layout. Made sense. Who knows?

"You pay and pay until it's covered. Money and violence keep secrets, period. And just like in *The Godfather*, it's not personal. Hey, *personally*, I'm sure Jack was great at parties." A polished white open gash of a mouth spread across Win's face, and a stupid smirk across Victor's, who was fading, hanging on, not for long.

"Father Joe forgot where he came from. Got too top-heavy to hold himself up. Too many debts unpaid. Somebody collected. The hot shit Kennedys and their friends cursed themselves, three ways. They forgot where they came from, they thought they were bullet-proof, and they asked for it."

Victor, resigned and with just a glimmer left, said "*They*, Dad? What friends?"

"Jack, then Bobby, with King in between."

"Dad, their 'curse' is us. We killed them. It's us."

The sweat soaked into his jacket as Win considered another payment, due any minute now. He could barely look up from the floor.

It was sad. The smiles were all done. Win would be going through this again, soon, to prepare to pass the business on. And he was back to rehearsing, for the now necessary next time.

"Couple pros from Europe, one of 'em a French Connection guy, one Chicago, one out of New Jersey and the rifles in from Brooklyn, the Big Apple contribution, according to legend. But who made out, in the end, was us."

Win bore down on his son, quickening, anticipating the sound of the finishing footsteps in the hall.

"Jesus, Halliburton's Texas home and grown and still kickin' ass in another century, for Christ's sake. All because some oilmen went back to the ranch, pulled the boots on, ponied up, and went after that East Coast, New England, oyster eatin', pig roastin', sailboatin', Yankee son of a bitch. Why can't y'all just eat beef? Drive big cars? *Don't you understand? How difficult is this?*"

It would soon get plenty difficult for Win, more so for Victor.

Win felt he could handle it, if he got out of the office. Now.

Victor could only blather "Dad! Dad!..." as Win left the door hanging, passing the others in the hall, all so purposeful with heads up and gloves on, coming hard. He hit the cross corner by the elevator and vomited. It wasn't the whiskey. Wiped his eyes first, then the rest on a hankie that nearly stuck to the wall when he slapped it there. He wheezed, caught himself, straightened up.

And Win thanked God for Katherine, called Kit by everyone before she could crawl, at Win's insistence. The line of succession needed to be rearranged, and today's unraveled loose end clipped. It was a new world after all, not all about the fathers and sons anymore. It was about who could get it done, and who could live with the awful truth.

The name Kit Annie Racklin would look as good, even better, painted on the glass doors.

It was raining, still nearly an hour until dawn, when they pulled up on the north side of Elm Street by the storied green grass, sloping up to the trees and *de facto* hunters' blind; the legendary wooden picket fence. Not the photo-famous original, but every slat repaired or replaced over the years as the whole plaza had been restored to replicate the vintage look from its famous day. Hardly any signage or sculpture to indicate what had happened there, but the nearby museum dedicated to the event had adorned the street with a big 'X' Marks the Kill Shot. Victor, still flying from booze and roofie, was out of the car and held up, under each arm, by hirelings' hands. He saw two others, blurs front and right. He heard more behind him.

Once before, back in the '80s, another intransigent oil heir walked this way, and that time they delivered the classic two behind the ear and the rest in the mouth message that crime gangs send to warn potential rats of certain fates. This time would be more of a re-enactment, like what those shooting-blanks Civil War buffs get all hot about. A lot like that, but a more *ammo vérité* version. This time, Jimmie, thoughtlessly wearing a new suit and pissed off about getting it wet with the rain and other things, held out his arm and shot a .22 into Victor's throat, just about where it'd nick the four-in-hand in an imaginary necktie. The balled fists darted up to his chin in reactive defense—damn, just like in the famous home movie that guy filmed, right over there. They say some local boys kept first generation undoctored prints in secret spaces, locked file drawers, wall safes...Brought 'em out for fun on movie night.

Errol had begged off this assignment, got a pass for services rendered, so it was wideload sweatshirted Bert reaching toward Victor's back and burying another .22 between his spine and right shoulder blade. It knocked him forward, still in his carriers' arms, lolling, looking right, and behind the big gaping Colt barrel pointed over his eyes, in a haze of a man, he saw his whole life, right up to that moment, then started left to run away from it, and they let him go, and he saw the whole rest of his life in a flash.

The Colt was aimed just above Victor's right temple, and the frangible bullet entered there, started coming apart and taking the right side of his head with it, and blew a hole the size of a softball out the back of his skull, a red blood, white bone and gray brain halo flowering like a firework until it misted and dissipated and floated to the street. The straight press would never detail the mirroring of history in the wounds, but a familiar breeze would blow word around, and the proper societal order of who's who and what's what would be maintained. The two Berettas would be broken down and scattered, but the Colt had been in the Racklin family for many years, and the good old boys would carefully wrap and box it for safe-keeping. They'd be prepared if it ever became necessary to finger a suspect and finally solve this ghastly, ghastly murder of the young oil scion. Yup, the rest of them would hook Win up and hoist him aloft in a second if something went wrong.

There's your curse for you. Apparently, it's catching. Infective.

And once daylight laid itself over the rain, and the coroner's crew was free to pack him up, the rest of Victor Racklin was carted away and on to Parkland Hospital, like another son of privilege so many years ago.

Osvaldo Veciana answered the phone and dealt with listening to Win Racklin explain their working relationship. Goddamn cigars.

"You know what I'll do to you, or what I'll have Errol or a hundred other guys do to you. You get the package I sent?"

Veciana had received the photographs. Portraits of Victor, before and after.

"I want to buy cigars. I want to buy you. I want you to do it for the money."

Veciana looked down at his shoes. "I'll do it."

His salty sweat and tears spotted the shine.

"I'll do it. For the money."

Veciana dripped and listened, acquiesced, and acknowledged Win with "You'll be here before Christmas, yes."

And as he said "I'll be ready," he remembered.

He hung up on Win, but held onto the phone.

The Texans, carrying some festive boxes and bags, left Veciana's store for the big, black car and bounded into the driver and right rear passenger seats, easily seen from fifty yards back, where one man fired up the old midnight blue Chevy and the other rode shotgun, literally. They were still saving the cigars for later, outside. G had readily traced them to his own Jersey neighborhood, and often conferred with Mr. Veciana about, oh, let's say the weather, and the big wind from out west.

"This vendetta thing over something he didn't actually do, like, fifty years ago, I don't know, it's got me queasy." Willy checked the rearview, edged away from the curb. Queasy was a rarity for him.

"Remember the Lord…and His vengeance. And all that."

"It's house rules now. He couldn't let it be, and he knocked on *our door*. He's asking for it, Will. He didn't *do it*? He *feeds* on the sins of his father. And what about a little 'when in Rome' for us? What we're doing has a little more local flavor, no? Reap what you sow, I say. Let the sins visit on him."

"Rome, you said? What about Errol, the noblest Roman of them all? He deserve this?"

"Nah. Reminds me of you, Will, like he's made out of knuckles. How about we offer him a job? Listen, get close, ride right up, squeeze 'em to the shoulder, see what kind of wheel man he is. Be fun to watch. And we're not gonna pop Racklin, I know. Let's be sensible."

G laughed at how long he had taken to come around to sensible.

Stella had helped in that regard with her pre-Yuletide gifting, featuring those crispy form-fitting gloves from the Hell's Kitchen Army/Navy, along with a spanking new leather spring-loaded blackjack and NYPD-issue telescoping baton she got from none of your business.

Stella wanted in. And that was—not the least, but exactly—what they should do.

"I'm sure these'll serve us well," she said. "Merry Christmas."

G knew she'd bought 'em with all that tip money. Classic toys, but not even one to, in the parlance, 'lock and load'. He got the message: no pistol play; no guns-go-bang-bang; cool down, boy. Way to go, Stella.

She was quiet, a couple beats too long. He took a look at his friend, saw her trouble, and joined her, gallantly allowing his eyes to tear, wet, and shine, too. Only to keep her company, of course, while they considered the scumbag Win Racklin.

"Hey, Stel, it's you and me and Will, we've got this guy," G said. "Ah, the fearful symmetry."

"One of your favorites." She looked down. "William Blake," she said. "Yeah, yes, all that 'Innocence and Experience'." She looked up. Eyes still a little damp, but burning bright, for her friend. "Love him."

◇ ◇ ◇ ◇ ◇

Willy was pacing the cowboys' car, laying off a little but right behind. "He's a big Texas oil guy. They got away with it because they kept their wits, you understand? Didn't get crazy. The biggest deal of all time. Learn a lesson. They did it for the money."

Whining is so unattractive; G's especially.

"*But we're the home team.*"

Willy sighed. Weary eyes on the road, foot harder on the gas.

G settled.

"OK, Will, fine. For the money. But Jersey style. Run 'em off the road, and after we knock him out, I'm picking his pocket."

CUCKOLD

by John Hayes

Chief assassinated!
Saw it on TV
was number two behind it?
seeking power and prestige.
No way
it had to be
a communist conspiracy.

The spouse?
No way
it had to be
a communist conspiracy.
Those guys scheme all the time
nearly as much as the CIA.

A cuckold?
No way
it had to be
a communist conspiracy
unless, perhaps the cuckold worked
for the CIA.

BOILER ROOM GIRL

by R.J. Spears

He was on her like an octopus, all writhing limbs, overheated, and wanting. Being cramped into the backseat of his Beamer didn't make the efforts to extricate herself any easier. In the moonlight, she could only see the dim sheen of his eyes and the sweat on his forehead as he loomed over her.

"Are all you east coast guys this fast?" Carly asked with a slight chuckle, trying to disarm the escalating situation with a little levity, but he was having none of it.

"Come on, you know you want it," he said in a husky whisper as he pinned one of her arms against the seat.

She grunted as she tried to free her arm, but he had eighty pounds and almost six inches on her. Plus he was on top giving him all the power. When she wasn't able to free the pinned arm, she brought her other hand up, grabbed a handful of his hair, and yanked.

"Bitch," he cried out, batting her arm away while pulling back a meaty fist, ready to launch it into her face. Just as he was about to bring the hammer on her, a loud knocking sounded at the back window. He stopped.

"Hey," a voice came from outside the car. Carly used this distraction to her favor and brought her knee up in a vicious arc into the man's groin. His mouth opened and closed like a fish gasping for air, his face contorting in pain as he fell off of her into the space between the seats.

Carly reached above her head, while turning over, and grabbed the door handle, pushing the door wide open. As she reached outside, a hand clutched her wrist and yanked her out of the car. She went with it, rolling across the dirt road. Something in her wondered if she hadn't just gone from the frying pan and into the fire. At least she was out of the car and away from that asshole. She'd deal with the next situation as it came at her.

The next situation leaned over her a second later. It was a woman in her late 20s with medium-length dirty blond hair, wearing a dark, sleeveless dress that had a '60s retro style to it. She also wore a concerned look. Before Carly could say anything, the car revved to life and with the door still open, it pulled away, sending a spray of dirt back onto Carly's face. She shook her head, knocking away the debris, and jumped to her feet in time to see the tail lights disappear across the bridge

"Asshole," Carly shouted into the night.

"Men are pigs," the woman said.

"Yes, they are," Carly said. "Total pigs." She ran a hand through her hair and exhaled loudly, then patted the pockets of her jeans. "Shit, he has my cell."

"Cell?" the woman asked.

"You know, a phone." Carly pantomimed holding a phone to her ear while trying to tamp down her exasperation. "Now what the hell am I supposed to do?"

Carly finally turned and looked at the woman. She didn't look as big now that Carly was standing eye-to-eye with her. "Hey, I'm glad you came along when you did. You saved me from getting my lights punched out. Maybe worse." Carly spun in a gentle arc, scanning the surroundings. "What are you doing out here? I don't see a car."

"I…I…" the woman stammered for a moment, "I'm in the same boat as you, a guy abandoned me here." Silence filled the air between them.

"You don't sound like you're from around here," the woman asked, shivering and hugging herself tightly. "It's so cold."

Carly didn't think it was cold. The day had been muggy and hot, but maybe the adrenaline rush had her blood flowing a little faster than normal. "I came in from Ohio last week. A friend of mine from college lives out here."

"And that guy?"

"My friend took me to a party. Just a little fun on a Saturday night. We met a couple guys. One thing led to another. My friend goes and leaves me at the party where I don't know anyone. This jerk seems nice at first and offers me a ride back to my hotel, then…well, you know the rest of the story."

"Don't I."

"What's the story on your guy?"

"He's just a man I know. He's in state politics. Nice, but married." The woman paused for a moment, looking into the darkness. "But not too married, if you know what I mean." They shared a knowing glance.

"How come he left you here?"

The woman's face fell into a frown then shifted into a question mark.

"I could use a smoke," Carly said. "Do you have a cigarette?"

The woman unsnapped her purse and water seeped from the seams. When she pulled out a pack, water dripped off it. When she turned the purse over, water literally poured out of it.

"Sorry, these are soaked," the woman said with a puzzled look on her face, tossing the pack onto the ground. "Where do you go to college?"

"Ohio State. I'm in Poli-sci, sort of. Or organizational communication, depending on how I feel at the time. What about you?"

"I'm just up for the weekend for a party. The guy who…who left me here organized it," the woman said distractedly, but came fully back to the discussion. "I work in D.C. We help new candidates get their footing. Setup campaign operations. Things like that. We just helped a guy run for mayor in Jersey."

"Sounds fun," Carly said.

"It is. Not as much fun as a big national campaign."

"Presidential?"

"I worked on one last year. We…" she stopped for a moment and coughed once. "We, my three closest friends and I, we were called the 'Boiler Room Girls' because we worked in this really hot room. We were responsible for sensitive 'hush-hush' stuff." She put air quotes up with both hands. "Anyway, we worked on a run for the White House, but it didn't work out the way we wanted though."

"How so?"

The woman started to answer, but broke into a coughing fit, unable to catch her breath.

"Are you okay?" Carly said, approaching the woman.

"Yeah," she said, but her voice became hoarse and breathy. Her color was bad, too.

"You need help," Carly said, moving closer, but the woman rallied and stood a little taller. "You're shaking like crazy," Carly said, an edge of fear in her voice. "Are you sick or something?"

"No. No," the woman said, clutching at her throat. "Something's not right, but I don't know what it is." She looked past Carly and past the bridge into the dark waters of the pond, her thoughts a thousand miles away. Her body quickly transitioned from troubled breathing to gasping for air as if her throat started closing. She looked at Carly with a panicked expression, not understanding what was happening.

"I'll get help. I can run into Edgartown," Carly said, leaning in towards the woman until she caught an offsetting combination of odors—pungent seawater and the sickening sweet smell of dead fish—causing her to pull back. "Yeah, yeah, I can do that."

Carly spun away and started to jog up the road, but turned back to take another look at the woman who was now down on all fours coughing up water. Lots of water.

Carly felt a different kind of fear rise in her. Not the panic that comes from being in a tight situation, but a fear that caused goosebumps to run up your arms. The fear from the bump in the night. She quickened her pace.

She really didn't know the area at all having only been driven around the island during daylight hours. So, she stumbled along for about half a mile before she saw a house and sprinted for it only to discover that no one was home. She jumped off the porch, heading back to the road. A part of her wanted to run back to check on the woman, but another part of her wanted to just get the hell out of there.

She fell into an easy but quick rhythm. In high school, she had ran track and knew how to pace herself but the fear kept pushing her past her comfort zone. That, plus the pack a day habit she'd picked up in college was her causing her own breath to become labored.

Just past another half mile down the road, a set of headlights appeared and she felt a sense of relief flood over her. She stepped off the side of the road and waved her arms frantically, hoping that the driver would stop and not freak out at her wild gestures.

When the car got within 50 yards of her, its red and blue roller flashed on and the cruiser slowed, coming to a stop just beside her.

"Officer, you've got to help me. There's a lady back at the bridge…"

A deep male voice in a thick Boston accent cut her off. "Ma'am, you're going to have to slow down some and take a breath."

Carly tried again, but only slowed her pace marginally. The voice cut her off again as the door of the cruiser opened. "Ma'am, have you been drinking tonight?"

"It's not about me," Carly said, almost screaming. "There's a woman back at the bridge. She's sick. She can't breathe. Maybe it's asthma or something. We need to get back there now!"

The officer stepped out of the dark and into clear view. He wore a crisp brown uniform which had a small cloth badge that said 'Deputy Sheriff' with the name 'Locke' sewed-on just above one of the pockets. He started to ask a standard battery of questions, but panicking, Carly cut him off. He finally capitulated and headed back to the cruiser. "Get in the car," he said reaching over and pushing open the passenger door.

"Hurry, please," Carly said, "That lady looked really bad."

Deputy Sheriff Locke was in his late fifties with a fine head of bushy black and gray hair and a face that had seen too much of the sun. He hit the siren and the accelerator almost simultaneously. They made it back to the bridge in only a fraction of the time it had taken Carly to get down the road. The only problem was that there was no woman there.

The deputy sheriff scanned his spotlight from one side of the road to the other. They exited the car and searched the area, but only found a small puddle of water in the dirt.

"She was here. I'm telling you, she was right here," Carly said in frustration.

"Do you know where you are?" Deputy Sheriff Locke asked.

"Yes, Edgartown," she responded.

"No, not really. Edgartown is back that way," he said, pointing a thumb back over his shoulder. "Sometimes, and it is rare, some strange shit happens around here."

Carly shot him a frustrated stare.

"This is Chappaquiddick. You know? Teddy Kennedy. Mary Jo Kopechne. 1969."

Carly felt an involuntary shudder pass through her body and her knees went weak. A wave of dizziness washed over her, sending her to the railing of the bridge for support. She steadied herself there for a moment, closing her eyes. When she opened them again, she was staring directly into the dark water. Something flashed below the gently lapping waves. She could make out a car, partially turned over, its headlights piercing through the murkiness. Just for the briefest of moments, she thought that she saw the woman.

The woman desperately clawed the back windows of the car as it shifted in the water, drifting in the current away from the shore and out of view. The woman's mouth moved, but no sound made it out of the depths. The lights of the car winked out. The dizziness that came over Carly just moments earlier became a tidal wave, pulling her under its blackness. As her knees buckled, she went down, feeling as if she were slipping into the chilled water.

Years later, she would tell her friends that she was never more afraid in her life than she was in those few milliseconds as she went under the dark waters of unconsciousness. She told them she felt like she was drowning.

NO MORE WAR REDUX

by Walter Giersbach

Kyle got back from Afghanistan on Friday, but he didn't call his grandmother till Monday. "I'm home," he announced. "Army said there's no more war. I could go home."

"Kyle?" she asked, and Kyle wondered if she was trying to remember his visit before he was redeployed. Or she might have thought about the first time he was sent to Iraq.

He interrupted before she blurted something that might embarrass her. "Could I stay with you? Awhile? Till I get a job, get my feet under me?"

Granny Kate knew homecoming was tougher than war. After her two years in Korea, she told him, she was shocked to encounter civilians encumbered by wheelchairs and overweight people huffing along out of breath.

"You're always welcome here! You know that. Now, how are your folks? You saw them, didn't you?"

"Dad's coughin' up blood from the lung disease. He's gonna need a lawyer more than a doctor. Doctors want cash. Mom, well, she said she'd rented my old room to a college kid. Pays by the month. Said she thought she'd told me, and that I'd like the kid when I came to visit."

"Oh, Kyle," she said. "I know things have changed. It was different when I was a donut dolly, driving my truck and taking coffee to soldiers in the detachments. We had benefits then. So did your uncle, after Vietnam. There was an insurance policy when he didn't come back."

Her words sounded hollow against the reality of layoffs at the mill, home foreclosures creating a ghost town, the grim looks on his friends' faces.

"Where have you been staying?" she asked. "Since you came back."

"Remember my old place on County Line Road? Been stayin' there. Roof leaked last night, but it ain't worth the trouble to fix. Bank's gonna come and change the locks when they take over. Who needs a roof if no one's home?"

"Guess we're plain foolish going to war all the time," she said before they ended the call.

Granny Kate's letters had been a lifeline when Kyle was in Ramadi and Basra, Kandahar and Kabul. His sergeant and platoon were like brothers, a family to rely on. They ate dust and MREs as they walked through valleys of death single file. He would come back from patrol knowing Granny Kate understood what soldiering was all about and why death had meaning in war-time.

Then Kyle told a captain at the hospital in Kabul there was static in his head, like a radio that wasn't tuned right. The doc ordered him to stop goldbricking and haul his ass back to his unit. Now, the telephones and car horns, the fire sirens and yak yak yak from friends were really getting on his nerves, like a toothache that wouldn't go away.

It was time to start his own war.

He wiped the oil off his .38 Smith & Wesson, sighted through the chambers, and then cleaned the pistol for the third time. Funny how people listen when you have a gun pointed at them. Didn't matter if they were some Afghan wearing a sheet or a banker saying, "Sorry, we're taking your house away." They always listened when you had a gun.

When his cell phone rang, he said softly, "Yeah?"

"Kyle Callahan? This is Caroline Kennedy."

"I know you?"

"I don't think so. My father was Jack Kennedy—President Kennedy—and I've been calling some of the American troops who've come home. You know, just to say thanks and make sure everything's okay. Bunch of us—Alec Baldwin and Cameron Diaz and others—we're calling veterans."

"Much appreciated, Mrs. Kennedy, but you know times are tough."

"I know they are. I see the news—and, you know, I talk to people. Senators and such."

"Fact is, I'm going to shoot some self-righteous bank manager."

"Oh, please, Kyle, don't do that. I know tragedy. My father was shot, and Uncle Bobby, too. I could go on and on. There was Mary Richardson Kennedy, who just hanged herself."

"Who?"

"I was telling you about the curse of the Kennedy family. Mary was Uncle Bobby's daughter-in-law. She got fed up with everything and simply checked out. My whole family is under this dark cloud."

Her words confused him. "It's just that the static in my head gets so bad sometimes. I think I've been cursed, too."

"Have you tried this thing that works for me? You close your eyes, breathe in through your nose, hold it, and then breathe out through your mouth saying, 'Everything's under control.' Do that a few times and it'll slow down your brain."

Kyle was intrigued. "That really works? It's yoga or something?"

"It sure works for me. Sometimes, with the kids and all, I get so down in the dumps I'm ready to quit."

"Don't quit, Mrs. K. You're an important person. And that Kennedy curse? That's crap. It's like saying there's some kind of supernatural conspiracy."

"Do you really believe it's all coincidence? The curse?"

Anger colored his voice. "I don't believe in curses. I just said that about me and why I was going to shoot some S.O.B. Everybody's equal in America and opportunity always knocks. Else what was I was fighting for?"

"Thank you," the voice said. "Your words have helped me. Now, I have more calls to make, so just remember to breathe in through your nose and out through your mouth."

"I know. And say 'Everything's under control.' Got it."

Later that night he wanted to call Mrs. Kennedy back and tell her the breathing trick was working. Tomorrow, he'd say, he was going to wake up sober, shower and shave, and go look for work again. Then he noticed Mrs. K's area code and telephone exchange were the same as Granny Kate's upstate. He suspected that wasn't Caroline on the phone.

He wasn't sure who he'd chatted with, but he did feel calmer. And if it was her, he could believe he'd helped her shake off this family curse nonsense. He just wouldn't tell anyone about their conversation or how close he came to going ballistic.

DEBTS OF
THE FATHER

by Zoe McAuley

Bridget first saw the odd man at an airport. He was rooting through the Duty Free alcohol in the passengers' lounge, sniggering at the melodramatic descriptions on the backs of the bottles. He caught her eye as she ploughed towards the coffee counter, already jet-lagged from the first stage of her journey. At first, his clothes were what made him stand out—he dressed like a hobo escaped from a Ren Faire. Then it was his height, for he was gangly, everything stretched a little long, a little wrong. In the end, it was everything about him—his pasty-pale skin, his razor-boned cheeks, his rolling movements and oily eyes.

As she huddled over her cardboard cup, Bridget's eyes kept drifting back to the odd man. Other passengers walked by, even pushed past him, without a flicker of a glance in his direction. She began to wonder if she was hallucinating him. After all, she had been travelling for some hours and would travel for several more before she arrived at Cape Cod and the family compound. She wondered if her cousins would drag themselves across the country so slowly. She doubted it. Sometimes it seemed like everyone but her owned a private plane.

The name of her flight caught her attention. A pair of pilots were strolling through the shop, joking about the job ahead of them. The odd man looked up too and smiled a crooked smile, stepping closer. With spindly fingers he plucked the co-pilot's hat from his head. At once the two men stopped. Bridget expected raised voices, but the co-pilot seemed frozen, his eyes glazed and loose, like an abandoned puppet. The pilot had paused as if waiting for someone. The odd man arranged the hat on his own head and stepped up next to the pilot. The conversation picked up again, as if never interrupted. The pilot did not seem to care that his companion had changed his face and his clothes and had gained a thick Irish accent. Nor did he notice his colleague left zombie-like in their wake.

Nor did anyone else.

Bridget shuddered. Perhaps it was just fear playing tricks on her. She hated flying. She had been to too many funerals with closed coffins or worse, empty coffins. Well-meaning acquaintances insisted that flying was the safest form of transport.

It wasn't if you were a Kennedy.

Staring at her hands as they trembled about her coffee container, Bridget was suddenly very sure that she did not want to fly anymore that day. She stopped caring about getting to the family party on time. Twenty minutes later, her plane ticket was cancelled and her train ticket was bought.

Later, she would feel foolish when she checked up on the flight and found that it had arrived at its destination without incident. Then she remembered those spindly fingers pinched about that hat and was glad that she had given in to her frightened whim.

She saw the odd man again, behind a pharmacy counter, processing her medicine. She decided not to take it. Then he was driving a taxi loitering outside her office. She decided to walk home that day. At her favourite bar, he was serving drinks that she refused to drink. At first, the sightings were weeks apart, but soon she was spotting him almost daily, among crowds of shoppers or drivers in stopped traffic.

For those first few weeks, she said nothing, self-conscious about the paranoid adjustments she was making to her daily activities. But when she found him in every mass of people, she confided in close friends and kin and was met with raised eyebrows, smirks and dismissals. Perhaps it was stress, suggested one sister, perhaps she needed to get away from the city for a while.

The idea took hold of Bridget, but not for the reasons her sister suggested. She sat alone in her apartment, mulling over the five occasions she had spotted the odd man that day, stationed along her well-worn paths through her working day. She was predictable and that made it easy for him. But if she wasn't, if she went away without warning, she might be able to lose him. She could spend a while unwatched.

She hired a car at dawn and left her boss a voice-mail. After filling the car with supplies, she drove without direction, taking turns as whims grabbed her. On empty roads it was easy to be sure that she was not followed and if she did not know her destination, the odd man could not predict it. Though it was winter, the mountains drew her in, snow-wrapped pillars of isolation. She drove for three days, sleeping on the back seat, before spotting a place letting out luxury cabins in the peaks. Ignoring their warnings of the cruelty of the weather, she took the key and ploughed up the steep roads.

The cabin was modern and warm, once the heating had a couple of hours to do its work. She moved her groceries into the cupboards and her clothes into the drawers. Then, when she was well-settled, she fell into the expansive bed and slept.

The hiss of a boiling kettle woke her some hours later. After a few bleary minutes, she remembered that kettles did not operate themselves.

And that the cabin did not have a kettle.

Bundling clothes on top of her pyjamas, Bridget quietly picked up her baseball bat and crept towards the kitchen. The light was on, but she could see no one. Maybe it was her imagination and a faulty memory. Bridget stepped into the room.

"It was a good attempt, I'll grant you that."

Bridget shrieked and spun to confront the voice behind her. The odd man rested inside an alcove, his long fingers wrapped around a steaming cup of tea. She waggled the bat at him, but he did not flinch. She considered simply laying into him with it without another word, but his nonchalance took the heat out of her fear and anger.

"Who are you and what the hell are you doing here? This is private property," she snapped as fiercely as she could.

"Would you like some tea?" he said, jerking a thumb towards the kettle. It was a battered old thing, with no place in a luxury cabin.

"Or are you too American for that? Forgotten the good a cup of tea can do you?"

"Just answer me."

"I will do, but I'll do it sitting around the table, if you'll kindly stop waving that stick at me," he said and took slow steps around her and to the table, settling himself down. He waved at the other chair. "Care to join me?"

Something infuriating in his voice made doing anything else seem utterly unreasonable. Bridget sat down, resting the bat against her leg just in case.

"Great, so now we're sitting," she said. "Now will you answer me?"

"Aye, I will. I'm an old family friend. Was a friend of your…" He squeezed one eye shut as he calculated. "…great-great-great grandfather, Patrick Kennedy."

"What?" Bridget said flatly. She knew who he meant—the first of the Kennedy family to emigrate to the United States. She also knew Patrick had died in 1858. She was too worn out for jokes. "Don't give me crap like that. Just answer me, dammit."

"That's just what I'm doing. It's not my fault that it's not the sort of thing you people believe anymore. I'm surprised you've even managed to see me, to be honest. Most of you don't. Makes it easier for me. You've been a tricky one to catch."

"What the hell are you saying? And why are you trying to catch me?"

"Oh, to kill you."

Bridget leapt out of her seat, swinging at him with the bat. He leaned back almost casually and watched it swing by, catching only the mug of tea. The ceramic cup smashed against the wall, splashing hot liquid over the wallpaper. The odd man sighed.

"Now, there's no need for that. It'll do you no good, even if you hit me. I'll just be back later. There's no getting out of it. Just sit down again, dear."

"No!" she shrieked. "You're threatening to kill me and you think I'm going to sit down quietly and chat about it? You're crazy! I mean, obviously you're crazy, but you're really crazy if you think I'm going to calm down."

"See, this is why it's easier when you can't see me. I could have just done you in. I'm being considerate, you know, by trying to explain first. I thought you'd like to know why you have to die," the odd man said, reaching out for his tea and finding it gone. Spotting the sodden patch of wall, he snorted and bent over to scoop up the ceramic fragments. Dumping them on the table, he curled his finger through the detached handle and muttered at the shards of pottery. The fragments leapt back into place around the handle, reforming the mug. As Bridget gaped, the cracks smoothed away until it was whole again, the floral patterning unmarred.

"Hope the kettle's still hot," the odd man grumbled.

"What the hell? How did you do that?" Bridget demanded, threats of death momentarily forgotten. "Was that a trick? You're doing magic tricks again, aren't you?"

"Of a sort. None of that sleight of hand guff, mine are real enough. Hell's bells, you saw me switch with that pilot and realised I was something odd. Don't come over all shocked now. Look, here's the short of it: your great-great-great-grandfather sold me your soul and I'm here to collect."

"Are…are you a demon?" Bridget whispered, wondering how she had come to be saying such words in all seriousness.

"Not quite. I'm one of the Aes Sidhe. We're a few steps up the ladder from demons." At her confused expression, he rolled his eyes and snapped, "I'm a fairy, alright? I hate saying that these days. Makes me sound twee. Anyway, the story, would you like the longer version?"

"I suppose so…"

"Right then," the odd man said, stood and began to make another cup of tea. "It was back in Ireland and your old man was heading to the port, off to make his fortune in the New World. On the way though, he made the old mistake of sleeping on a fairy mound, so we did the usual, took him off to a party, messed with his head a bit. But we got to talking, too, him and I. He told me all about what he was hoping for over in this America. Now I'd been looking for a way in on this New World malarky for a while, given half the mortal population seemed to be upping sticks and moving there. So I figure we can help each other out. I offered to bless him and his line so that him and a certain proportion of each generation would be fabulously successful. He was keen enough on that, of course. But my price was this—I'd kill and claim the souls of a proportion of each generation, too. Both the lucky and unlucky descendants would be chosen at random, fairest way to do it, and any one of them could fall under both the blessing and the curse, if that's how chance dictated. He dithered a bit, but in the end he agreed. It was all sworn up and set in stone by the time he left for the ship the next day. So all this time I've been making your kin among the most powerful folk in the New World and I've been claiming my fee."

"I take it I fell into the unlucky category…" Bridget slumped back into her chair, balancing between disbelief and despair. "How could he make such a cruel bargain?"

"Ack now, don't be hard on old Patrick," the odd man said between sips of his fresh tea. "It was a different world back then. You'd expect to lose a few children in every family or to die young yourself. He didn't really think he was losing anything from it, and there was a lot to gain. The likes of him didn't have much chance of making it anywhere in life. Admittedly, you came off poorly, being doomed to die and not enjoying any of the fabulous success. But a deal is a deal and a soul is too valuable a commodity for me to give up over a little pity."

"So the curse? All the deaths in the family? That was you?"

"Yep. It was me tucked behind that grassy knoll. Me smothering them in their cribs. Me jumping out in front of cars and fiddling with their chemicals. And I tell you, I am one lousy pilot."

"When are you going to stop?"

"When I run out of Kennedys, I suppose. I'm on to a good thing here. There's been some fine juicy souls over the years. You're not half-bad yourself, if that's any comfort to you. Perceptive and stubborn. I like it."

"Well…thank you, I guess…" Bridget sighed and stared into the fake grain of the table surface. Suddenly a thought bubbled up into her mind, like a drowning swimmer breaking the water's surface. "So you make deals with people? We could make a deal. One where you don't kill me."

The odd man chuckled gently, "See, this is just what I was talking about. All right, let's give this a go then. I already own your soul, so you can't bargain with that. I already own your children's souls, too, so that's another old favourite out of the way. What else have you got to offer?"

"Well…I…" Bridget stumbled over her words. "What do you want? Money? I could probably get hold of some money. I mean, you know the kind of resources my family has to hand."

"That I do, since I helped them get the lot. Don't you think I could have such things if I wanted? I'm interested in something a bit more powerful…mystical, if you like."

"I have…I have nothing like that."

"I know," he said kindly and reached out to pat her hand. "But it was a nice try."

"So…how are you going to kill me?" she whimpered.

"Oh, I'm not a cruel man. Just go back to bed."

The mountain rangers didn't find the body until the following spring, when the unusually thick snow had cleared. Their verdict was that the cabin had possessed some subtle structural weakness, imperceptible to all but the most thorough examination, and that under the weight of the increased snowfall, it had buckled, killing Bridget Kennedy in her sleep. They concluded that there was nothing anyone could have done to prevent the unfortunate accident and buried her with her family.

THE
PLUTOCRAT

by John Hayes

I sit alone in The Poor Boy Saloon
needing money for a vigorous drink.
Downed my last B&B before noon.
I hated staying last night in the clink.

A Kennedy enters holding his honey
buys me a bourbon which I down in one swig.
I offer my thanks and borrow bus money
wink at his date who wears a red wig.

"I'm off to my office to get my week's pay,
before my boss gives it all to my ex."
"Cheers," he says. "I got divorced yesterday,
The best things in life are whisky and sex."

The rich man grins as her wet kisses flutter.
I wonder, does he know she's my mother?

BODY DUMP

by Mike Sharlow

I didn't realize how much the decision to talk to a stranger could change my life. It was like the decision to get on a sled to go down a hill called "Suicide." At first it appears to be fun, an exciting scary ride, until things become dangerous and far more frightening than fun. Jumping off the sled could be just as deadly as riding it out.

For almost a year since I had gotten the design job in Bishop, which was about twenty miles from Riverton where I lived, I drove past Bill's Twin Corners Tavern without ever stopping for a drink, probably because I really didn't drink that much anymore. It was faster taking the county roads back and forth to work instead of the interstate, and Twin Corners was one of those very small towns I drove through.

Now that I broke up with my girlfriend—or rather she broke up with me because she said I was commitment-phobic which was true—the last time I had sex was about a month ago, so I figured it wouldn't hurt to stop at this hopping little bar on my way home from work. There were always quite a few vehicles parked outside. Who knew whom I might find in there?

Almost every barstool was full. I found a seat on the left of a black guy who was talking to two white guys on his right. I'm sometimes prejudiced, but I'm not racist. This area of Wisconsin and probably more so this town of Twin Corners was quite "conservative," which where I come from equates prejudice with racism. When I was growing up, there was only one black family in Riverton and probably not another black family until Madison. Now, there were more black families than anyone other than the census knew, but they still probably represented less than ten percent of the population.

The black guy was as big as any guy in the bar, so nobody was going to fuck with him, and the two girls behind the bar didn't have a problem serving him. An older gray-haired white guy stayed at the other end of the bar. If the climate wasn't obvious by the farmers wearing caps advertising farm implements or the hunters in camo, then the TV's at both ends of the bar tuned to the GOP channel said it all.

The black guy's friends, who were white, were of average height and a bit on the skinny side. They looked like most of the blue-collar guys in the bar except for their longer scraggly hair.

I waved at the bartenders, and one of the girls came over.

"Cranberry juice," I said.

She looked at me cockeyed and winced like I had just blown a wad in her face. "I'm not sure we have cranberry. I'm new. I'll check."

I smiled and nodded at the black guy next to me.

"Hey, brother," he said. "Don't drink?"

"Can't."

"They have cranberry juice," he said as the bartender came over with a tumbler glass filled to the brim.

"Can I have it on the rocks?" I asked her.

"Oh, sure, of course."

"She likes you," he said. "You make her nervous."

"I'm not sure I want to fuck her, but I do want a glass of cranberry juice," I said.

"Why can't you drink? You on that shit for alcoholics that makes 'em sick?" He smiled like he wasn't trying to offend me.

"You mean antabuse? No," I said. "I have back problems. I don't like to drink on my pain meds."

"I know what that's like," he said as he drank from his tapped beer. I wondered if his beer and the empty shot glass were taking the place of his meds, but of course it wasn't unusual for people to mix drinking and drugs. In the past I had done it myself. Now I thought it was stupid and risky. Statistics seemed to bear that out. A serious functional drug addict understood limitations, which meant that the limits were no longer visible and quitting was a distant goal. This was me, and if I wanted to survive this, I believed I had to exercise some discretion. Getting addicted was inevitable but dying wasn't.

Addiction to Tramadol was similar to morphine; therefore, apparently, the withdrawal was also. There have been a couple of times when my supply of drugs had run out before I was able to buy more. This rarely happened, but when it did, I plummeted quickly into the cold, dark, lonely despair of withdrawal. The physical and psychological elements were inseparable. My body became subject to a torture that felt like flesh slowly separating from bone. At first my mind slowly lost control of my body. My muscles twitched, and I squirmed to find comfort. I tensed my body, hopelessly trying to find control of my arms and legs. My mind told to me escape, to run. Ironically, it was my mind wanting to escape my body. Finally, when the drugs were back in my body, there was no better relief. The internal chill was replaced with a calm warmth. All was right in my world. It felt like I had the answer to the key of life, and that was like the security of the womb. I wondered, "Who wouldn't want that?"

"You know what?" I asked.

"What it's like to have pain? To take pain meds to get rid of it? Joe Moen," he introduced himself.

I shook his hand. "Nice to meet you."

"What kind of meds you on?" he asked.

"Tramadol."

"Right, trammies. I have to take quite a few of those to get high," he said.

I was waiting for him to sidle up to me and ask me for some. They were in my car. I never went anywhere without them. I tried to remember if I locked my car.

"You ever do Fentanyl?" he asked quietly.

"No. I've heard of it." I read somewhere that it was a hundred times stronger than morphine.

"I know where to get some," he said in the same discreet tone. "You have forty bucks to chip in?"

I figured forty dollars was the full price. I knew that he just wanted me to finance his high. I wanted to experience Fentanyl, so I was okay with this. "I have forty to spare," I said.

"Cool," he said. "Let's go boys, we're gonna pick up the He-Man."

"He-Man" was slang for Fentanyl. One of his cohorts knew exactly what he was talking about and jumped up from his barstool. The other guy looked confused but soon figured it out.

I followed Joe in his rusting silver-blue Ford Aerostar minivan. I knew the vehicle because when I was married I owned one. His looked like a piece of shit like mine did. Because of vehicles like that, I now only drove Toyotas or Hondas. Presently, I owned a Civic.

Joe led me to a clean, quiet, old neighborhood on the north side of Riverton. The street was lined with big elm trees on the boulevard. I had lived in this town all my life, and although I knew where I was, I don't think I had ever been on this street. Riverton was a little less than sixty thousand people, and I rarely came upon a street I had never been on, or remembered being on. Joe walked into a brick house in the middle of the street. It was a story and a half with a steep fairy-tale roof.

As I waited, I wondered how often the police patrolled this neighborhood. A long time ago I lost the illusion that drugs were sold in back alleys and tenements. Riverton had disenfranchised neighborhoods and low income housing, and although drugs were found there, they were also found everywhere else, like this Norman Rockwell neighborhood.

In less than ten minutes, Joe came back out and drove away. I followed him to a different part of the north side to an eight-plex by the railroad tracks. His neighborhood was five minutes away from the one we bought drugs in. It was not as clean or as well kept.

Joe lived in apartment four with one of his two friends. The apartment smelled of old sweat and dust. The beige carpet hadn't been vacuumed in quite a while. The apartment had Spartan furnishings. The black leather couch, the only place to sit, was worn and cracking like skin with bad eczema. He had a fairly new TV with a good-sized screen, likely over forty inches, directly across from the couch. Oddly, I didn't notice it until Joe flipped it on with the remote, and some nature show came on.

Joe's friends took the couch, so I sat on the floor. Joe came back from the kitchen with scissors, a roughly six inch by six inch piece of aluminum foil, a plastic straw cut in half, and a disposable lighter and sat between his friends. He dug his hand into the front of his pants and pulled out the Fentanyl. It was a topical patch, supposed to be applied to the skin. I knew by the equipment Joe had, this wasn't the route we were taking. After carefully cutting into the patch, he squeezed a dribble of clear gel from it onto the foil. He handed the straw to his roommate and heated under the foil, as his roommate slowly inhaled the vapors. His roommate held it in and collapsed into the couch. Joe did this for me and his other roommate before taking a hit himself.

After my hit I found myself lying on the floor with my hands behind my head. I stared at the nature show and felt a symbiosis. This was a great show. I felt no pain, physical or mental. The euphoria had given me complete comfort.

"Well?" Joe asked as he looked at me.

"This is perfect," I said.

"Fuckin', right," Joe said and laughed.

Each of us took one more hit.

Maybe two hours passed. I wasn't sure. I was nodding from dreams to consciousness to somewhere in between. Then, I sort of snapped to, and I realized I didn't want to be there anymore. These weren't my kind of people. This really wasn't my scene. I wasn't a social addict. I saw the drug patch, the foil, and the scissors on the floor in front of Joe, and I decided that I wasn't leaving empty handed. I looked at Joe and the other guys. They were fluttering in and out of consciousness except for the one guy that hadn't done anything like this before. He was out cold and kind of pale.

I cut the patch in half and headed towards the door with my share.

"Heading out?" Joe asked with a sleepy, gravelly voice.

"Yeah, see ya," I said.

"What's it feel like to get high with a Kennedy?" he asked groggily.

"What?"

"That guy." He pointed at the guy who was out cold. "He's a Kennedy. You know, a 'JFK' Kennedy. A cousin or somethin'."

"Really?" I said but thought it was a bunch of bullshit. Although, why would he bother to mention it?

"Later, man," he said.

I closed the door behind me and fell into the cool night. I took a deep breath and felt glad to be alive on this Tuesday.

On Saturday morning, I turned on my laptop and went to the *Riverton Daily's* online newspaper. On the first page was the headline, "Two Charged in Body Dump." With a headline like that, I had to read the article. When I saw Joe Moen's name, my pulse increased. My anxiety reached a panic level. I kept taking deep breaths to try to calm myself. The article said that Joe Moen and Tyler Kretch would be charged with the drug-related offenses and possibly the murder of Bradley Kennedy. The article talked about how they dumped Bradley Kennedy's body along the river in Oneida Park on the north side of town. I knew this park was only a couple of minutes from Joe's apartment. The police were looking for Leonard Lorend, the guy that sold them the drugs. The article said that there was possibly one other individual involved. That individual was me.

I tried to remember every detail of that night. Everything was fairly clear until we did the drugs. I was sure that I had never told Joe my last name. I never told him where I worked or what I did for a living. He did see my car. Unless he or his roommate had photographic memories, I didn't think he knew my license plate. Hopefully, they didn't recall one letter or number. I wondered how long it would take before the police would find me—if they would find me. I tried to go about my Saturday normally, but it was impossible. I ran my usual errands, but whenever I saw a police car, I felt panic. My life was on the verge of imploding. I felt the cloud of impending doom hanging over my head. I had to do something to fix my life.

The events of the night reeled through my mind on an obsessive loop. I was pissed off at myself for taking Joe Moen's offer. I didn't sleep well. On Sunday morning I got out of the shower and stared at myself in the mirror. I felt a surge of anger, and I slapped myself in the face, twice. "You stupid fucker!" I yelled at myself. I was always somewhat self-loathing, like most addicts, but I rarely resorted to physical punishment.

I called in sick to work on Monday. Work was a manufacturing plant where I was a designer. What I designed and what they made really didn't matter at this point. I had worked there less than a year and only recently became eligible for the 401k plan, but I had almost seventy thousand dollars in the plan from my previous employer of 15 years. I kept it there because they used a local financial institution to handle their retirement plan, and they weren't charging me any fees to leave it. I also liked the idea of being able to walk into the place where my money was kept. Now, I hoped the convenience of my money being local was going to pay off.

I hadn't gone back to my previous employer since I quit. I went to work for their competition. I felt weird and nervous walking back through the door, and my predicament exponentially increased my feelings.

"Hi, Monica," I said. She was the receptionist.

"Hey, Mick, what brings you back?" She acted like she was glad to see me.

"Retirement plan stuff. Is Harry in?" Harry was the human resources guy.

"Yeah, does he know you're comin'?"

"Talked to him this morning," I said. He was expecting me. "He better be here," I thought.

Harry was in, and he gave me four pages of paperwork. Most of it was signing my name, which I did quickly and erratically.

"I'll fax this over today," he said.

"You mind if I just take it there myself?" I asked. "It's downtown on Fifth Street, right?"

"Yeah," he said. "I have to have Dan sign these forms. I'll see if he's available." Dan was the owner/general manager.

"I'll come with you to say hello," I said. On my last day working here, I went to his office to thank him for giving me the opportunity and say good-bye, but he had already left. At the time, I knew he was pissed that I was leaving. I had started as a lowly grunt in the shop. I became a supervisor rather quickly, and then Dan pulled me out of the shop to be a designer. I was a lead designer when I left. I repaid him by leaving for a better paying gig. Now I needed his signature, a signature that was likely the difference between freedom and prison.

"Dan, Mick is here to take care of his 401k," Harry said. "We need your signature on a couple of forms."

"Hi, Dan," I said standing behind Harry.

"Hi, Mick," he said, glad to see me and standing up to shake my hand. "Decided to come back to us, huh?" he joked, but I knew there was an element of hope behind it.

"I'm leaving town. I got a manager position in Durham, South Carolina," I lied. Then I wasn't sure whether Durham was in North or South Carolina. Ah, fuck it. It didn't matter.

"Good for you," he said. I think he knew I was lying. Once again, it didn't matter. Soon enough, he would know the truth.

I took my 401k papers to the Riverton Trust Company. It was an older building in downtown Riverton. I stared out their tall windows at the small city below where I had lived my entire life. I knew I would miss it if I left. It was almost a half hour before someone was able to help me. My perspective of time had changed. The importance of time had changed. I wondered how close or far the police were to finding me. I was in a race and didn't know where my competition was.

Laurie Hanson, a girl I went to high school with, worked at the trust company. I never knew her very well. We had a couple of classes together. "Hi, Mick," she said and led me back to her office. She was wearing a tan skirted suit. Her face was average looking, but she had big tits and muscular calves which made me fantasize about her momentarily, even in the predicament I was in. I thought about my primal urges for a second until she interrupted. "What do you want to do with your money? Did you want to roll it over into a Roth IRA?"

"I want to cash it in," I said sadly. "I need the money." I wanted her to feel sorry for me. I made eye contact with her until she blushed and looked away. I knew I had her.

"Okay," she said.

"Can I get a check today?"

She paused then said, "Sure. I have to take out federal taxes. Do you want to take anything out for state?"

"No," I said. I knew I had made her day more complicated and maybe even a bit difficult by asking her for the check today.

"Can you come back in a couple of hours?" she asked.

"Thanks a lot, Laurie. I really appreciate it."

In a couple of hours, I came back, and she had the check waiting for me. I took it to my bank and told them I wanted to cash it. "It's from the Riverton Trust Company."

"Since it's from there, it should clear by tomorrow," the personal banker said.

Throughout the remainder of the day and into the night, I checked my bank account about every half hour to see if the check had cleared. Just before one o'clock in the morning, I logged on again and saw it had. I took a hit of the Fentanyl so I could sleep, and as I lay there, I was amazed how smoothly everything had gone so far, but I knew at any point, when the police figured out who I was, it would be over. I could have run the moment I read the article, but with only a few hundred dollars in my pocket, life would become very difficult very quickly. The only way to do it was the way I was doing it.

I called in sick again to work the next morning after taking the last shower I ever would for a long time in this country. I packed one small bag and waited for the bank to open while I drank a cup of coffee and watched MSNBC. I felt bad that I wouldn't be able to vote for Obama in November, but that was what I deserved for being party to the death of a Kennedy.

How the Mighty Have Fallen

by Raymond Gallucci

Forever bound by Fate in dying young,
No more the heir apparent and the king,
Again the son and father live as one.

The prince was coronated by the gun
That ended Camelot's awakening.
Forever bound by Fate in dying young.

Coincidence that cords The Sisters spun
Were meant to terminate their spools of string?
Once more the son and father live as one.

Was brother of the king condemned to run
Like salmon in the fall instead of spring?
Forever bound by Fate in dying young?

Will uncle of the prince be ever done
With Curse that Chappaquiddick yet can bring?
At least the son and father live as one.

Combined, their spans of life correctly sum
To length to which most thankfully would cling.
Forever bound by Fate in dying young,
At last the son and father live as one.

LAST WILL OF LITTLE ROSIE

by Paul Lorello

I made Sister Agatha go blind this morning. She had it coming for her obstinacy. Trying to get me to eat when I'm not hungry. It'll be temporary, of course. Just long enough for her to write down what I dictate from here on in. They'll say it's a miracle, and they'll probably canonize her for it. But really it's just cheap theatrics. I've got to amuse myself somehow. Life here at the cottage is bland as a biscuit.

Which reminds me: Teddy's coming by in a few minutes. I hope there's at least a bit of uncertainty in him about me. I've always wanted my death to come as a surprise. But this is just as good. The family name is now a punch line. And the last remaining comedian to deliver it is coming here to bid farewell and beg yours truly to undo it all somehow. Like I said, just as good.

Sister Catherine is sobbing in the garden. Y'oughta consider the lilies of the field, Sister.

She's terrified of me, poor thing. I gave her boils on both hands for making that noise in her throat when she looked at me. I'm getting sloppy in my old age. There was a time I could send a brown recluse down the dress of a debutante and then just sit back and watch the frolics. It certainly made those disgusting parties bearable. They never looked once in the direction of little Rosie the spastic. I think it was around the time of John's second bout of jaundice that the basis of their revulsion of me shifted from the corporeal to something beyond. And that's when they had me fixed by that quack surgeon who thought he could rid the world of witchery one scoop of grey matter at a time. For the record here, meticulously documented by our crusty-eyed Sister Agatha, I had nothing to do with jaundice. It is classic, though, isn't it? Like old, rabid Salem: An act of God brought about by the sins of the father and suddenly the superstitious lot singles out the little odd girl in the village.

Which is more miraculous: That all of nature should be arranged for misfortune to taint every member of the clan at every step, and strike them when they're at their highest? Or that alcohol coupled with a fermented morality was responsible?

Here's the answer: Whenever the pattern could have been set right, it wasn't. Now does that sound like the price you pay for cutting out a chunk of a girl's brain, all because you couldn't bear a female with real power in the family? Hate to disappoint, dearies, but I ain't that petty. Life's been dandy apples for yours truly. I really mean that. You show me another member of the family with this much freedom. Sure I've had to put up with their monthly visits; twelve times a year they've cancelled plans in order to come out to the cottage and see their sweet, drooling Rosie. If Catholicism's taught us anything, it's how to supplicate.

Sister Agatha is scribbling like crazy in her cell. They'll question the miracle. So as proof, let her write that Teddy is here now and he's wearing a sweater the color of raw pork. How could Sister know that if she can't see him? I guess one of the others could have tipped her off. Alright, more proof. Sister Catherine's menstrual cycle is heavy this morning. Let them discuss that at Sister Aggie's beatification hearing.

A little about the gift. It's like moving pieces on a chessboard. Only zoom out until you can see that there's not one chessboard, but zillions of them, all with pieces you can move. You can feel them as well. You know what every piece desires. You feel the holes in them. Understand? But you can't be everywhere at once. No one with the gift is capable of orchestrating a true miracle, or a curse for that matter, for to move one piece is to move a thousand and then a thousand more. No, I'm afraid it's been nothing but chintzy witchery from yours truly all these years.

Teddy leans over and whispers close to my face. Good boy, he hasn't had a drop. Just coffee.

"Rosie, darling," he says in his pink, padded voice, "we've worked hard. All of us. Eunice started the Special Olympics in your honor. Remember? Jeannie does so much for the cause. All of us who… who live still…we do everything we can."

I giggle and point to his sweater. I'm not playing. It really does amuse me.

Teddy says my name so softly, it's almost as if he doesn't believe I'm real. And that's when I hear an echo I've been hearing in the dark for almost forty years now.

Ted's been trying to hide her from me. All the mental energy focused on that very task is what's been holding him back his whole life, only he doesn't realize it, poor old sot. Every now and then he lets his guard down, and her gaze burns through me like salt. That's when I close my eyes and sit very still and hear a tender voice calling him back to the depths.

I felt them die over the years. All of them. (I know what it's like to lose a chunk of your brain.) But I haven't known a *living* thought like this in quite some time.

"We've tried," Ted whispers. "All of us. We've tried to make up for our shortcomings."

I close my eyes. I sit very still.

The metal twists.

"You've set us on the path of right. Bobby had some good in him. I had good in me. We tried."

Suddenly I'm snorting up gobs of burning water into my nose. Her hair does a scarf dance in the weightless night, caressing my arm. Exquisite.

"Jeannie is a good woman who shouldn't be made to suffer."

And I walk away from the wreckage, from the clawing desperation of that sweet, soft hand, thinking that here is the sacrifice needed to end the curse once and for all.

"Surely our sentence has been served."

And the memory play ends in a cat's twitch.

I look at his gorgeous face. The best and kindest of the lot. And this is when I finally pronounce the curse, the only real curse ever to befall Camelot. I hit him with my sugar smile. "Teddy will die in four years," I say, and hold up my fingers. "In August, the year of Our

Lord, two thousand and nine. Sweet Jeannie will be at his funeral. Make sure she has Kleenex. That's the end of the curse." End of my little curse, I mean. Not the Kennedy curse. There is no Kennedy curse.

I don't know where I heard that knowing the date of your death can be a curse. It doesn't have to be. But to a guy like Ted who only has four years left, it's a kick in the ass after living so long and never quite getting it right. I don't tell him that Eunice will die that same month. Let Jeannie miss Eunice's funeral so she can sit on the deathwatch with Ted and see the curse to its fitful end.

The family won't have to worry about this last will of mine going public. Someone on our end will work with the Vatican to keep it quiet, for sure. The boys in Rome will enjoy all my worldly possessions. Daddy always knew how to handle the money.

I'm dying now. Sister Agatha can clean her eyes and have breakfast.

ACCIDENTS HAPPEN

by Nick Andreychuk

Ever since Danny's parents died in a car crash, accidents seemed to follow him like an unwanted shadow. Not that Danny himself was accident prone, but rather, misfortune seemed to extend to everyone around him. As if putting up with the loss of his parents wasn't enough, the poor dear had to live with the unshakable feeling of being cursed, which was reinforced by his distant relation to the Kennedys on his mother's side. (Yes, *those* Kennedys…)

Of course, Danny never discussed his feelings with me. But a grandmother knows. Why, the mood swings alone were a dead giveaway. One moment, he'd be full of joy, and then someone'd get in an accident and he'd be mopey for days. It never failed, just when he seemed excited about life again—*Bam!*—another accident.

The first one was actually an unsettling déjà vu. Right after his parents' funeral, Danny rushed to the church's washroom, where he was violently ill. I sent my nephew, Johnny, in after him to see if he was all right.

"He's not doing too well, Auntie," Johnny said when he came back out. "He said we should go to the cemetery without him. He'll meet us there soon."

The cemetery was within reasonable walking distance, but I wasn't about to leave Danny alone on such a sad day. I was supposed to drive Johnny, his wife Martha, and some of the in-laws in my minivan though, so I gave Johnny my keys.

Danny must've been really sick because I sat outside that washroom for over half an hour. When he finally came out, he was so surprised to see me that I knew I'd done the right thing. We walked to the cemetery hand in hand.

The scene that greeted us there was, well, let me put it this way—I still have nightmares about it to this day. My minivan was wrapped around a large oak tree not fifty yards from my son's freshly dug grave. We soon found out that Johnny and Martha were both dead. Fortunately, the other passengers only suffered bumps and bruises.

Even now, I get chills thinking that could've been me.

Not all of the accidents were as tragic as the first, but none of them could be considered minor, either. There was the time when the mailman broke his ankle in a hole by our front porch. Danny had dug the hole to plant a tree he'd bought me for Grandmother's Day, though why he covered it with that green tarp I'll never know. And the poor mailman got hurt for nothing—I had Danny plant the tree elsewhere since he'd dug the hole right in the middle of my normal route to the sidewalk.

Another doozy was the time Danny left our heavy wooden ladder leaning against the wall next to the front door while I was out grocery shopping. The nice young stockboy who carried my bags home got quite the bump on his head when he stepped into the house ahead of me.

I could go on and on about the drained swimming pool, the lamp with the faulty lightbulb, the golf balls on the stairs, and countless other accidents. But the simple fact of the matter was that friends, relatives, and strangers alike just weren't safe when Danny was around. I count my blessings every day that my daughter-in-law's family curse has never caused *me* any bodily harm.

Yesterday, tragedy struck. It was Danny's birthday, and he'd asked me to bake him his favorite extra-chocolaty chocolate cake. But his girlfriend, Angela, had wanted to surprise him with a romantic dinner and a homemade cake of her own. Who was I to argue with young love? So, I let Angela have free rein in my kitchen while Danny was out looking for a job. (The poor dear still hadn't found a job, even though he'd graduated some years ago).

The accident happened just as Danny came home. He entered through the back door off the kitchen. He must have seen something that I hadn't, because he screamed for Angela to put down the electric mixer the moment he saw her.

Sadly, his warning was too late. The instant she switched on the appliance, it sent a jolt up her arm strong enough to knock her off her feet. I don't want to get into the gory details, but I heard the paramedic say over his radio that she'd been "fried like a bird on a wire." Turned out the electrical cord had been frayed…from rubbing against the counter's edge or something.

To be perfectly honest, I never did like that girl, but Danny worshipped her. She was very materialistic, always wanting Danny to buy her more, more, more. I wouldn't be surprised if she'd secretly wished me dead so that she could marry Danny and get her hands on the sizeable inheritance I'd leave behind.

And now she's dead instead.

She'd told Danny once that she'd like to have her ashes tossed off the edge of the lookout—or I should say, *make-out*—point where she and Danny first kissed. When we got there, Danny asked me to toss Angela's ashes over the knee-high guardrail for him, on account of his fear of heights.

I took the urn's lid in my left hand and flung the ashes out into the wind. I jerked the urn really hard, mindful of getting ashes on my freshly ironed blouse, lost my grip, and dropped it over the guardrail. Fortunately, it landed in some scraggly bushes that were just within reach.

As I knelt down to retrieve it, Danny suddenly screamed out in surprise.

I looked up in time to see him rushing at me with outstretched arms. He must have thought I was falling and reached out to grab me. He tried to stop, but he'd built up too much speed. He ran right into me and flipped over my back. It was my turn to scream as he flew over the edge to his death far below.

The poor dear—his curse finally caught up with him…and now I have no one left to leave my money to.

Non Compos Mentis

by A. A. Garrison

"I thought I was someone else, someone good."
—Lou Reed

John considered the agent's question, sipped his complimentary coffee, and took a deep breath. The interrogation room smelled like it looked.

"I met Abe through his dog," John said to the unsmiling FBI agent, and immediately began to explain. "It happened at my house, up on Eagle Ridge, in the mountains. I saw movement out the window—a dog, German shepherd, out in the road and dragging a leash. I was busy, with the President coming to town and me on the campaign, but there was that leash…so I went outside. The pooch came right up, friendly as anything. I took him in, and resolved to drive him around that afternoon, after I finished up with work.

"When the time came, I packed up the dog and went canvassing my neighborhood. Eagle Ridge is all mountains and bends and such, sparse, so no one up there really fraternizes like a traditional neighborhood. A consequence of geography, I guess. Point is, I didn't really know my neighbors, so I met a lot of new people as I tried to find the dog's owner. Including your man, Abe Kennedy.

"He lived a couple miles from me, so his was one of the last places I hit. I'd seen Abe's before—one of those octagonal bungalows that were all the rage in the seventies, looked like a chintzy flying saucer. It spoke of wealth, and I'd admired it. Guess I could buy it if I wanted, now, but it's not so attractive anymore.

"There was no car in the driveway, but I went to the door anyway. I knew right off the bat something was up. I knocked and waited, and there were noises—locks unlocking, three or four or some ridiculous amount, like we were in the middle of Compton instead of the mountains. That was creepy enough, but then the door flew open to Abe, looking like I'd pulled him off the toilet. I introduced myself as his neighbor John, and then asked, real meek-like, if he had a dog, getting right to the point—he looked like he'd wanna get to the point. Instantly, he told me no—with no accent, mind you. Before I could say more, the door closed and the locks were snicking shut. I left faster than I'd come.

"I didn't like him, obviously—no one wants a door in the face. But there was more to it. The whole encounter, it just left a sour taste in my mouth, I can't really elaborate. I guess I know, now, to trust that instinct.

"Well, I did the rest of the neighborhood, and no one was missing a dog or knew whose he was, so it looked like I'd just become a daddy. I decided I'd print up some 'found dog' posters the next day and throw them around town, but I didn't really hold any illusions about finding the owner, so much that I bought a big bag of chow and a food bowl and other goodies. And that was that, I thought. I named the dog Barrett. It seemed appropriate—vaguely German, very shepherd.

"But, no. The next morning, just after breakfast, I got a knock on my door, and there's none other than Abe Kennedy—except it *wasn't*. See, I could tell right away he was different, just by his look, the small muscles of his face. He was still the same person—tall and fortyish, with that long Anglo face, even wore the same clothes—but it was just his…demeanor, his whole temperament, that was different. And it was *better*, pleasant, a world apart from when he'd grouched to his door the day before. I was puzzled, but then he introduced himself, and things went outright odd.

"It was his accent, see. He spoke with a pronounced English accent—a flourish—and even though I'd only caught that one brusque 'no' from him before, it was an *American* no, the kind that slaps you in the face. So there's the first two quirks, but then came the clincher: he asked if I'd seen a dog, German shepherd, probably wearing a leash.

"I started thinking it was a joke, right? That, or Mister Kennedy was some flavor of psychotic—which ended up half true, as it were. I stayed cool, though, and just fetched Barrett to the door, pretending yesterday'd never happened. I was too happy to unload the dog to read into it much. I'm not one for pets, especially not then, when I was gearing up for the President's pit stop at the convocation center.

"After re-introducing myself as John, I handed Barrett over—whose name was actually Garfield, I learned later. Abe, he damn near burst into tears. Funny: the hard-ass from before, he wouldn't have cried if he stepped on a nail, and here he was, blubbering and rubbing noses with the dog. I was intrigued, so I asked Abe inside for a cup of coffee, but he declined, darkening—though not in a malign way, just defensive, like I've seen victimized women do, and I respected that. The guy obviously had some species of problem, so I just accepted his many thank-you's and we parted ways. I noticed he left on foot—weird considering the kind of house he lived in. I asked him, from my window, if he wanted a ride, but he declined that, too."

John began to say more, but was interrupted by the tall black spook with the hard face. "About your work, Mr. Lincoln," the agent said to John. "We've checked into President Hopper's campaign, and you aren't listed, as a paid member or a volunteer." A dubious pause. "Care to explain?"

John nodded airily, parrying the accusation. "Yeah, I can explain," he said, and drained his coffee. "It's not wholly legitimate, but I guess you guys don't really care about that, in light of the present… situation." He cleared his throat though it didn't need it. "I'm not listed because I'm only on unofficially, in the campaign's underbelly—the dirty work, see. I am—or *was*, I guess—what's called a 'shill.' Basically, I pose as your average John Q and go out proselytizing for the President's reelection, mainly online, over the internet. I sit around for hours a day on different bulletin boards and discussion groups and the like, offering subliminal support for the Pres while tearing down anyone who drops an unkind word—even if they have a point, I'm sad to say. A guerrilla tactic, crude but effective. There're probably fifty guys like me. The conspiracy nuts would have a ball. I go out to rallies, too, both for President Hopper and the opposition, working the crowds in a real-world version of the scheme. Plus I uproot the opponents' signs. Heh. Yeah, dirty, but the other guy has people doing the same, so I guess it balances out. The pay sucks, for what it's worth." He regarded the agent, over the paper-littered table. "You aren't going to, I dunno, *arrest* me, are you?"

The agent glowered. "Back to Abraham Kennedy, please," he said, still stern as a train's cowcatcher, but satisfied regarding John's employment, apparently.

John reached for his coffee, remembered it was empty, and retracted his hand. "Okay, so I'd just given Abe back his dog," he said, a little wearily. "A day goes by, I'm working hard, shilling for President Hopper—then I remembered the dog food and stuff I'd bought. Short of having another lost dog fall into my lap, I never planned on getting one, so I figured I'd take the stuff down to Abe's—which was pointless, of course, since I would end up with Garfield again. But I didn't know that at the time.

"I went that evening, and when Abe came to the door, it was a repeat of my first visit, him looking stormy and distracted, like he'd bite my head off if I got too close. But, before I could say anything, recognition spilled over his face and he lightened into Good Abe. He greeted me with his cheery English lilt, though without the chipper he'd shown when picking up the dog. I cut to the chase and handed over the dog stuff. He was very grateful, and it was then his turn to invite me in for coffee.

"His place was as nice inside as out, very spic-and-span, with knickknacks and trinkets scattered around, dish gardens—a wife, I thought. He led me to a quaint kitchen, and poured coffee from a pot already made up. We drank, making small talk, and Abe still had that guarded air to him, maybe from something grating on him. I almost didn't ask about his one-eighty and whatnot, but the questions nagged and nagged, so I just came out with it.

"He responded with this long, unreadable look. I started to apologize, thinking I'd offended, but he just waved me off and said, 'You have a right to know. It's good someone in the neighborhood does, just in case.' Well, I was captivated after that, and he didn't disappoint.

"He stared dreamily through his kitchen window as he informed me of his 'condition,' looking like he was reliving a war story, I thought. I'll paraphrase: he was a classic split-personality. There was Abe One, the pleasant English fellow I was talking to—the *real* Abe—and then Abe Two, the cheerless jerk I'd encountered when I'd come around with the dog. Abe explained that he'd grown up in England—normal—but in the late eighties his parents had suffered a fatal accident and so he'd moved abroad, to put it behind him and unstress. His 'other' self had cropped up shortly after, starting with what he'd thought were blackouts—from the trauma, you know. But these weren't blackouts, they were his Other, so much another man living in his head. 'The change' would come every week or so, he said, almost always when he was asleep, so he would simply wake up as Abe Two, losing a day here and there. And though it was very regular, enough that he could prepare in advance, there were exceptions, like his ill-fated walk with Garfield the dog. It explained why he didn't own a car, I remember thinking.

"He said he really didn't know much about his alter ego, other than that the man was a total ogre toward others, and was 'a Yank,' since he spoke with an immaculate American accent. Abe had discovered this by setting out a hidden camera and recording his other self. He actually showed me one of the tapes—he saved them all, like an anthropologist—and on it was the man I'd met when I'd first come by, contrary and squinty and mad at the world. The guy was ostensibly Abe, but *wasn't*—the change was so apparent, like an expert actor in character, or someone possessed. Profound. Anyway, all the guy—and that's just how I saw Abe Two, as another person completely—all he did was pace around Abe's living room and mutter random American-sounding words, which was typical, according to the real Abe. The guy didn't do anything but pace and look unhappy and eat peanut-butter-and-jelly sandwiches—was a *fiend* for P-B-'n-J, Abe said. He had to keep a constant stock of the stuff, or the other him would tear through the kitchen, hunting it as a junky would drugs. In other circumstances, it would've been funny.

"Abe fixed up another pair of coffees after the tape, and I could tell there was something more weighing him down. He spoke up before I could ask. 'I'm afraid my problem has worsened as of late,' he said. 'I received my bank statement today, and it would appear that the other me has made several substantial withdrawals. He's drained me, the bugger.' He sipped, and I saw his hand was quivering.

"It wasn't as bad as it sounded. Abe, who came from money, had a trust fund in addition to his checking account, and this would, at least, put food on his plate. But he was still pretty upset over it. His account would be replenished by the trust, but there was nothing keeping the other him from pulling an encore, so it was an ongoing thing. Worst was, he had no idea what the other him had *bought*. He couldn't find anything new in the house, which he found disturbing, since the Other had made off with nearly five grand.

"At that point, I thought of suggesting the obvious solution, since his other self was demonstrably whacko, yet smart enough to impersonate his counterpart. But, again, Abe beat me to it: 'I've tried having myself locked up, you know,' he said shamefully, probably having read the question in my eyes. 'It's remarkably hard securing a bed in a psychiatric institution, due to overcrowding. Preference goes to nutters too poor to support themselves, as opposed to nutters with a trust fund.'" John sent the agent a poignant look. "But Abe was a good guy, really he was. You all gotta understand, what he did, it was his Other, someone as separate from him as I am from you."

When the agent made no response, John continued: "Anyway, it was getting late and I had to get back to work, but before I left, I gave Abe my number and told him to call me if he needed anything. And I meant it—I was concerned. Maybe my job isn't the most respectable, but I'm not all bad. I paid Garfield a farewell rub-down, and left Abe looking a little better than I'd found him.

"A week passed before I heard from him again, and to be honest, I'd forgotten all about Abe and his doppelganger and his dog, since this was just two weeks ago, with the campaign going nuts in preparation for yesterday's speech—my God, was it just yesterday? Seems like ages ago. Well, anyway, I was in my office, shilling, when Abe called. I heard the trouble in his voice as soon as I picked up. I straightened up and asked what was wrong, but he wouldn't tell me over the phone, said I had to come see for myself.

"I had no idea what I'd find. Maybe the bungalow on fire or

blown up, or five thousand bucks' of peanut butter and jelly in his pantry. I don't know. Everything looked okay when I got there, but Abe had this grave look to him and I started expecting the worst, something in the neighborhood of a dead body. I again asked what was wrong, but he only led me down the basement stairwell, to a big metal door at the bottom.

"Abe gestured at the door without saying anything, as if I should understand its significance. When I shook my head, he told me that the last he'd visited the basement, approximately a week ago, there'd been no door, metal or otherwise. This didn't strike me as overly odd—so the other him had taken his bonanza and installed a door, big deal. But then I noticed the locks—eight of them, on the *outside*, all fitted with a quality combination lock. I understood then: the Other had claimed the basement.

"I asked if there were any other points of entry, but there weren't, and there was no arguing with that door. The thing had thick diamond-plating, reflecting funhouse versions of us. I knocked on it and it was incredibly solid, like Superman's chest maybe. I suggested some bolt cutters, but Abe had already been down that road. Short of some dynamite, the door wasn't going anywhere.

"We went upstairs for coffee, and Abe explained that he'd lost not just one day this week, but *two*, together. He'd gone to bed Monday and 'woken up' Thursday, that morning. It was his first blackout since he'd last been in the basement—Abe was an amateur photographer, and his darkroom was down there—and so he was sure his Other had exploited the extra time to install the door. We pooled our thoughts, fueled by two whole pots of coffee, and I got the idea to call around to local lumberyards and contractors and such, because the door had to be a special-order job, and weighed in the hundreds of pounds, and there's no way Abe installed it alone. Unless the Other could lift a gazillion times his body weight like an ant, *someone* had to have helped him. So we drudged through the yellow pages and called around, but it was a dead end. We even called the local hardware store, seeing if anyone had come in for eight hasps and combination locks, but they couldn't remember anybody. It seemed the other Abe had foiled us.

"It was a bad situation, and I felt as helpless as Abe. The subject just drifted off then, an awkward silence taking its place, so I started looking aimlessly around his kitchen. That's when a 'Hope with Hopper' magnet caught my eye from Abe's refrigerator. I pointed it out and we started talking politics, and it turned out Abe was all for the President, and that's how I got the idea to put him on the campaign. I figured it was something to at least get his mind off the money and the unsettling basement door, and he agreed, though without much fanfare. He couldn't do much, not having a car, but I figured I could give him a lift to the convocation center when the President made his speech, to pass out magnets like that on his refrigerator.

"So, the next day, I went down to the campaign headquarters for a bundle of handouts, then drove back up to Eagle Ridge to deliver them. I was kind of anxious driving over, I'll admit, because I didn't know what to expect—real Abe or other Abe? I'd already developed an aversion. Luckily it was the real one who came to the door, and I delivered the handouts and promptly vamoosed, since it was ten days to the President's arrival and I was already behind from going to the headquarters in the first place.

"He rung me again two days later, that Sunday, and I again heard dilemma in his voice. He'd made another discovery, he said, this time a suspicious receipt. He implied he wanted me to come over again, to 'make a proposal.' Over more coffee, Abe said that his Other had dropped by the day after I'd left, and the receipt was a slip-up on his part. Abe had found it stuck to his communal shoe, attached perfectly lengthwise as to be easily missed. The receipt was from Radio Shack, for nearly two thousand dollars' of Greek-sounding purchases, so we put our deerstalkers back on and made a call. We were lucky enough to get the clerk who'd serviced Abe's split. The man remembered Abe vividly, as 'the big pissed-lookin' feller.' According to him, the Other had come by cab, forked over a foot-long shopping list, and paid cash. I asked what the things on the list could be used for, but the clerk said they were components for a million different things. 'From computers to microwaves to pyrotechnics.' So, again, we were screwed.

"After I hung up, Abe had one more clue to share: the other him was apparently computer literate, enough to use the internet. I asked how he knew this, and he said his computer's browsing history had been wiped, which both supported the claim and crushed any hopes of investigating it. There was paper missing from the printer, too, so the Other had taken some things for the road. The plot thickened.

"I started to leave then, needing to get back to work, but Abe sat me back down, for his 'proposal.' He wanted to set up another hidden camera, except this time rig it to the internet—so that I could keep tabs on his Other. I didn't immediately answer. It was one thing to drive down to Abe's and lend him my ear, but to watch over him like a pet? I mentioned how I'm not one for pets. I said no, but Abe was insistent, convinced that his other self was up to something nefarious—and man, didn't he hit the nail on the head. Looking back, I think there was some bleed-through there, like maybe his Other's intentions had seeped over into real Abe's share of the gray matter. Anyway, I couldn't turn him down.

"As it turned out, Abe had anticipated my cooperation, and installed the camera earlier that day, overlooking his living room and the only door exiting the house. So, after I fielded the latest storm of thank-you's and went home, I was able to jack right in. I brought it up on my computer, and there it was, a washed-out view of Abe's living room, him in it, reading *The New Yorker* and nursing more coffee. Normally it would've been problematic to watch the feed while doing my internet work, but I happened to have a spare monitor, and was able to attach it additionally to my workstation, dedicated entirely to Abe. I only had to glance over to see what was up. Easy. Still, it didn't seem like it would do much good, even if I watched it twenty-four-seven—since it was in the *basement* that the Other was constructing his supposed doomsday device. But I'm a sport, so I humored the whole thing.

"Days passed, with the President's visit getting closer and closer, and I heard nothing from Abe, though I saw him regularly on my computer. It was sad, seeing him mope around his kitschy little house all day, reading or watching TV or doing nothing. He had no company, no phone calls, no wife, just him and Garfield, looking as bored as they probably were. But I guess I shouldn't talk, considering my life's not exactly salted with excitement. Heh. Anyhow, three days after I started the surveillance—just this last Wednesday—I got my first audience with other Abe.

"It was just as he'd said: Abe went to bed as one man, and woke up another, instantly recognizable as such. I only caught fleeting glimpses of him throughout the day, always just passing by as he went about his lunatic routine—until around seven or so that evening, when I saw him play across the frame, going out the door and into the night. I watched until I went to bed, but I never saw him come back.

"The next day, Thursday, I breakfasted with the local news, and that was how I learned of the burgled construction site and its missing explosives. At once, I knew I had my work cut out for me, because the theft was perfect justification for President Hopper's new security initiative—and just before his visit! As soon as I finished eating, I stormed all the local websites with support for Hopper, on the platform of the nation's continued need for stricter security measures, with the theft as evidence—great work, if I do say so myself. I made poetry of propaganda, so immersed that I completely forgot about Abe's transfiguration the night before, not remembering until after lunch.

"The deal was, I would contact Abe in the event of a blackout, so after I'd wrung all I could from the burglary, I gave Abe a perfunctory call. He sounded horrible, like he was hung over and had a cold, saying that whatever his Other had been up to, his body was sore as hell. I listened, but my head wasn't in it, because of work. What can I say? I like what I do."

The other agent, a flushed man in a suit too small for him, spoke from his post at the other side of the room. "Do you have recordings of this surveillance?" he asked in a strained, befitting voice.

John shook his head. "No, would've taken too much disk space. And besides, what good would it do? There's no question it was him. I mean, we've all seen the footage. There were a zillion cameras there, Zapruders galore."

The agent gave a noncommittal nod and returned to his corner. "Proceed, please."

John shrugged. "Not much more to say, really," he told both agents at once. "You guys know what came after."

"Refresh us," the black agent said. "For the record."

John scratched his head. "Well, nothing much happened after that," he said. "Abe had three 'good' days, him staying him and all, and I did my thing. Then Monday morning rolled around, yesterday, and that's when it all went to shit.

"I woke up excited, couldn't wait to see the Pres—in the flesh, you know. I felt like a kid. The speech wasn't until four-thirty, so I went about my normal morning. At my computer, I noticed that Abe was his evil twin again, sitting on Abe's couch with a big plate of P-B-'n-J and watching TV, which was showing the President. For a second I thought it might just be Good Abe having a bad day, but looking closer, I could see that bastard look in his eye. He was yelling belligerently, seemingly at the President on TV, spraying little eruptions of sandwich. I couldn't hear what Abe was saying to the President—the feed was video-only—but I'm sure it wasn't flattering, considering he waved a middle finger every so often. Abe's Other was not a fan, as we know now.

"It meant Abe wouldn't be handing-out at the speech just hours away, but what can you do? I brushed it off and went about my work, counting the minutes. On my other monitor, Abe continued heckling the TV—until around three-thirty, when he checked his watch, stood abruptly, and disappeared into the house, toward the basement. I barely noticed, since I was getting ready to go to the convocation center, but just as I was leaving, I caught him again. This time, Abe was carrying an attaché suitcase I'd never seen before.

"I only saw him a split second before he stormed out the door, neglecting to close it behind him—with Garfield inside.

"I knotted up when I saw the open door, conflicted—I knew I had to drive over and close up, so Garfield wouldn't get out and end up God knows where, perhaps in unfriendlier hands than the last time. I fought this, of course, with it being a little over a half-hour to showtime; but when I left the driveway, I turned toward Abe's.

"Just down the road, I passed a yellow cab with a tall fare—Abe. I wondered, distantly, if he was also on his way to the speech. Which he was, of course.

"The door was still wagging in the wind when I got to Abe's, but Garfield remained inside, along with a giant mess. The place was trashed, literally, with paper torn up and snowed all over the place—

the campaign handouts, ripped into a hundred angry pieces as if run through a machine. Then, on the far wall that I couldn't see in the video, there was an enlarged bust of President Hopper, riddled with darts and defaced with satyric horns and a goatee. Videos were strewn about, too, all President Hopper's old flicks. *Easy Rider* had been given the same ugly treatment as the poster, with Peter Fonda untouched. The TV was still on, hyping the speech I was now late for.

"It was then, in Abe's trashed living room, that it hit me. The locked basement. The radio junk, used in 'pyrotechnics.' The stolen explosives and Abe sore as hell. The Other's violent dislike of President Hopper." John snapped his fingers on each item. "And even though I knew in my heart it was true…I still couldn't accept it. I mean, Abe, the next Oswald? It was just too crazy, so I scrambled down to the basement, hoping it would be open so I could find other Abe's store of smutty magazines, or his Dahmer-esque dungeon of horrors, or his tunnel to China—*anything* but what I knew I'd find there.

"The big metal door *was* open, but inside was just what I'd scented upstairs: a darkroom repurposed into a maniac's bomb factory. The room was dominated by a big developing-table with a little clothesline hung over it, and it was covered with empty Radio Shack packages, and snips of wire, and dog-eared printouts offering instruction on how to construct a bomb—even a few sticks a dynamite, laying loose like hotdogs. Scattered around the room were more defaced likenesses of the President: a cardboard standup that had been decapitated, posters and movies and magazines. Was an action figure, too, riddled with pins like a voodoo doll. I froze for a good minute, like walking in on people having sex, before I scrambled back upstairs and called the cops. Then the shit hit the fan, and now I'm here."

John paused, fixing the black agent with the steeliest look he knew. "So, to answer your question, sir, *that's* how I knew Abe Kennedy was headed for the convocation center with a suitcase full of T-N-T." John pooled in his chair, exhausted.

For a long time, the agent wrote over his clipboard. "Thank you, Mister Lincoln," he said afterward, in a patronizing voice. The man holstered the pen and clicked off the tape recorder. "You'll be called upon to repeat yourself before an inquest, but for now you're free to go."

"That's it?" John said.

"That's it," said the one agent. The other one, across the room, stayed silent.

John stood dazedly from the table. He nodded a goodbye, then quit the cramped room, throwing out his coffee empty on the way. He thought of getting a fresh cup somewhere, but that would only remind him of Abe.

John feared the press waiting for him when he got home, but, miraculously, there was only Garfield. John walked him and fed him and gave him more attention than necessary, before fixing himself a dinner that went uneaten. When there was nothing left to do, John started for bed, even though it was just after dark.

On the way, however, he noticed his computer and its adjunct monitor, still displaying Abe's crime-scene living room. It was even more upset after the passage of all the police and technicians: muddy footprints, things turned over, the basement stairwell stitched up with yellow tape. The TV was still going, currently showing a commercial for soap. Nothing else moved.

After a moment of watching, John powered off the computer, detached the extra monitor, and put it out of sight.

KC

by L.L. Hill

Feathers ruffled, a black-headed seagull did a quick side-step on the balcony rail as a wind gust blew off of the churned grey waves. Islands to the north blocked the full force of the Atlantic winter storm.

"I'm just like you," KC thought, looking at the seabird. "My black head above a white windbreaker, grey chinos and grunge loafers. And I survive by looking for handouts and feeding on carrion."

Always too hard on himself, he sipped his coffee and winced. Even the muddy drink had a more acrid flavor. So much for rain water, collected and treated before flowing through a gold-plated coffee maker in a silver-plated timeshare on loan to him from a cousin.

His phone rang and he flicked it on with a polished fingernail. The gull lifted effortlessly away.

"Who let the dogs out, KC?"

"Pleeze, not now!" Kennedy Jackson Jefferson Carter, named after presidents of the United States and descended from two, had endured years of taunts as a child as the "Kennel Club". He had never minded "KC" though.

As a child the gibe had been annoying. Waking up this morning to putrid earth coating the front steps and this back deck was information that he had texted away to another cousin, who had obviously forwarded it to Joe, the current patriarch of the clan.

"Seriously, you didn't touch any of that crap, did you?"

"Of course not! I hosed it all down and then poured bleach all

over. Jen will probably have some dead plants to look at next week."
KC flicked the unit's monogrammed keys in one hand.

"My guess is that it was probably grave dirt, dropped by someone at midnight…"

"Probably, yes, there were no footprints and the soil was covered by the morning dew."

"Point is, superstition aside, grave dirt is loaded with bacteria from decomposition…"

"I didn't touch it. My hands were washed for five minutes after putting down the bleach." KC looked at a swelling on his hand. The problem with chocolate skin is that you could not see the red warning of infection.

"Are you feeling okay?" The concern sounded real.

"I feel like shit. I had a fire cracker 'accidently' fired at me yesterday, the same day that I got thrown out of the Archives as 'unqualified' and instead of jogging the beach this morning, I had to clean up a dead person and drink fucking bad coffee."

"Easy on the language, KC."

"Are you taping this? Add insult to…"

"To keep you safe! Did you call the police? Obviously you've provoked a response."

"And am glad to have done so!" KC paused to sip the horrid coffee. "No, I didn't call the police. What would I tell them that they could do something about?"

"Well, stay organized and share, and think really strongly about taking a break stateside."

KC was silent, twisting the key ring and watching the cloudy waves break and surge below him.

"KC, in just over a week, you've evidently located information that someone doesn't want publicized."

"Or someone thinks that I might if I look through enough files. I have to be realistic, Joe. You and I have both seen the police and the coroner's reports on Ken's death. It wasn't an 'accident' that he fell overboard while on watch as crew of a racing yacht, though the cause of death is described as 'drowning'. Neither the police nor the coroner seem to want to investigate."

"And you know that was to allow an investigation to go on

behind the scenes."

"Which hasn't happened. Nobody's investigated anything. And for viewing the files of an unsolved murder, Sir Harry Oakes, that is approaching its hundredth anniversary in two years time, I have been threatened and verbally abused, some of which was by government employees."

"What made you start with a murder almost a hundred years old?"

"An internet search, 'unsolved murders Bahamas'. It remains the biggest hit, though there are a number of others."

"That's a lot of interest to provoke from a web search."

"Wasn't the web, it was requesting and copying files in the Archive."

"I mean your interest in it, KC."

"Oh, well, I was looking for parallels, common features of unsolved crimes." The gull returned to the corner rail.

"Think about it, KC, almost a hundred years. Guy died when?"

"July 8, 1943."

"And is there a remote possibility that anyone who did it is still alive?"

"No chance, Joe, but that is part of the parallel, because great-uncle Jack's generation is also deceased, and Ken is the latest proof that some group doesn't like the family values."

"A group? How do you figure that?"

KC smiled as someone with Joe asked, "And what family values? I hadn't noticed any."

"Back to the parallel. It stands to reason that if someone wants to keep the motive for a murder almost a hundred years old quiet that it has to be an organization with current financial interests that would be threatened by exposure."

"Organized crime? That's hardly a secret organization. They would probably benefit more from the intimidation value of a big hit than from adding to mystery and notoriety by hiding the truth and killing anyone that asked too many questions."

KC breathed in and out slowly before answering. Out beyond the reef a fast powerboat approached the harbor, low and slow in the water. And the gull glared at him from the rail.

"KC," Joe prompted. "Still there?"

"Still here. Think about it. Ken went into the water, which destroys evidence like DNA on clothes. His body wasn't recovered for four days. A woman that said she had heard an argument on board was not named in the police report nor ever questioned again."

"Tell me something that I don't know, KC."

"I'm getting to the point, Joe. That's why I got to start my gap year in the sunny Bahamas, remember? Anyway, Ken also had what is described as a 'contusion' on his head. Wait, let me finish," KC said as he heard Joe inhale to speak.

"Sir Harry Oakes was found dead in his bedroom, covered in feathers, battered, with a hole in his head, not from a bullet, and physical signs that he had been killed somewhere else and moved back to his bedroom. The second to last piece of information is not common knowledge. Do you know what sort of 'contusion' Ken had?"

The answer came back slowly. "No, but a 'contusion' is just a bump or a scraped bruise, not a hole in his head."

"Maybe the coroner never looked or missed something. Back to Sir Harry. There were suggestions of a connection to organized crime because Sir Harry was using his position to keep casinos out of the Bahamas, and how important are they now?"

"Very, but I know of no rumors of connections to organized crime."

"Did you know, Joe, that I had already done three days of research on Sir Harry before I got thrown out for not being a graduate or a Bahamian researcher?" KC answered his own question.

"It was when I had started to research the Duke of Windsor and Wallis Simpson that I got thrown out."

"What are you suggesting?" Joe sounded intent and worried.

"As you noted, organized crime would benefit from a big hit. A family, the descendants of a murderer would probably not be happy about having a murderer in the lineage."

"I can't see that bothering the Royal Family. They've apparently got quite a few of those."

"No, the Duke disgraced himself by abdicating for a divorcee that had spent time in a brothel, according to some reports. Even if he had been Fascist, the Brits would have left him to ignominy. Fascists would have had a use for him."

The seagull leapt away on a gust. Joe was silent.

"But think, what would Fascists do to keep their plans for world domination under wraps? What did the First and Second World Wars get fought over? What was on the US agenda when uncles Jack and Bobby were assassinated?"

"Human rights and equality." Joe was terse.

"Yes, an unrelenting battle." The gull flew past and veered away.

"Did I tell you about the imam that tried to recruit me in my sophomore year?" asked KC.

"No."

"Well, he came preaching the line about a 'worldwide brotherhood' and returning to my ancestral religion. I let him talk to me a few times, and then showed him an article about one of his Arab predecessors, someone that was openly opposed to Africans as not human, just animals. A very Fascist ideology as well."

"He left, I take it."

"Didn't see him again for over a year. Not until yesterday in the Archives, in fact. Just after the firecracker and just before I got kicked out of the Archives."

"KC, I think that you should leave the Bahamas right now. Even though I can't see what Muslims and Fascists would have in common, it sounds like you've really stirred something up."

"What they have in common is hatred of Jews. Hatred is an easy emotion to exploit."

Feather stung behind KC's ear. His hand waved once and dropped to his side.

"KC, KC, you there? KC!"

Mountain of God

by Tim Lieder

To non-believers, it's just a little field behind a row of dead houses. The grass grows wild and the buildings rot from the foundations. No one lives on the block. If you see a man walking over, looking like he's going home, know his guilt and move on. Only the desperate may find and see the sacred among the crab grass and bricks.

If you watched from the adjacent alley you might see the two divine vassals, barely distinguishable from refuse. In the cold wind, they smelled like fish and sawdust. One was a woman older than her years with stringy yellow hair; her face caved like a dry orange. She held her head to take the sky and her eyes to the fallow ground. She leaned on a skinny yellow boy of indeterminate morality. The couple had been bouncing at walls all night. Their feet were bloody. They had avoided the communion of neon bars, candy stores and corners. In alcoholic puddles, they listened to feel fast cars and blue drivers.

"I was the valedictorian," he said. He was tall and thin without teeth. His air escaped ragged and soothing. The cheekbones suggested that a handsome nerd had once inhabited his body, before pimples, drugs and paranoia broke him.

"My son turned me in before they took him away. I hope they killed him," she said.

They were talking cycles in a conversation veering and lurching about: "My son turned fucker me in. My son fucker saw me taking my fucking medicine. It was fucking medicine. It kept me fucking alive. I kept fucking me alive. I was fucking alive and fuck my fucking son. Fucking didn't fucking think I deserved to live? My son. My son is fucking dead."

His words shot into his lucid. "I was the valedictorian. I gave the valedictorian address but the quantum creeps were in with the Trilateral Commission. I saw the way my girlfriend looked at me. She knew everything.

"You know why the world is fucked now. You know why you can't drink a glass of water—even bottled water, without drinking feces? You know why the ozone layer is going to burst wide! The trees are falling apart. Our father is in prison, hallowed be thy name. If you would only listen to reason you'd understand that Vincent Bugliosi lied. He even said that our father was 5'3" when everyone knows that he's five foot six. Sharon Tate died for your sins. Stop fucking around, man. The trees are falling. The Reagan corporate polluters are killing you. Your children will be born with the heads of fish. Your oceans will brown. Your skies will black.

"I was walking in the desert and I had a revelation. The sun was burning me and I was afraid. My tongue swelled and I could hardly breathe. I looked at feet and I saw a rock. I remember thinking in this insane way as I looked at it, 'Well, this is a good place to die.' I began laughing. I was so happy, until I walked out.

"Charlie walked out of the same desert a man of infinite joy and glory. When Sirhan Sirhan introduced Robert to apotheosis, Charlie blessed all the beautiful dirties. Allow Charlie into your heart. If you ever resist Charlie, you become just a Sharon piggy. No one ever listened to the dreamers. Their visions of hurricanes and earthquakes lay in shallow misery.

"Let's go to the mountains of god," said the boy.

"You remind me of my fucking son. I'd suck your fucking dick but I don't fuck Asian boys. Fuck. I told the judge that I wouldn't suck his fucking dick because if I fucking did that I could never be a respectable fucking woman."

"No. Let's go to the places where the roaches are beautiful and cigarettes taste like ambrosia. Let's go away from the Communists."

"My son. Fucking kid looked like you. Except white."

"My name is Adam," said the tall kid, "No one remembers that I'm a genius. The mountain of gods will open for us. The FBI's Al Qaeda branch can't kill the flowering."

She stopped to cough; first dry but then brown heavy phlegm. Her head stared at bricks. Her tongue picked at the gap in her teeth. Her hair swayed and just for a second, she looked as if she would cry. The wind tossed a Styrofoam container at her feet. She shivered and stomped her foot; the wind subsided.

"I can suck your dick if you give me five dollars."

"I don't have five dollars. They took it away."

"Bullshit."

"You're not one of them. You wouldn't understand. I was one of them but I deprogrammed myself. They wanted to give me pills but I go to the parties and I beat up the drinkers. I was a straight-A student until the federal government discovered that I knew how they were hiding Jesus Christ. The Israelis were trying to get me because of my Junior paper. The teacher almost gave me a B because of outside pressure but it was too good and he gave me an A-."

She swayed in the bright city lights. There was no moon. Acid rose to her throat but she held it. Her eyes opened round, yet the angels did not touch her hand.

AUM is Zen. The AUM Shinriko is the question to the answer. Listen and you'll hear Shinriko singing. Listen closely; the AUM walks behind you. Hear, oh suspicious ones. The AUM Shinriko loves its enemies; ready to give them a tasty nirvana. Japan was not big enough Aum; Aum must come to Vietnam. Everyone comes to Vietnam. Display the dreamy life in the grassy dunes behind the bleachers.

They were pushing chemicals. She needed to believe Adam because Adam was good. She might even suck his dick without payment but she needed a fix; the stores were locked so tight. Everyone put bars on their windows. The jerks yelled the same invocations. They called for whitey. They offered plastic bottles to the pavement.

"You hab not been to church," said the woman, "You hab to go to church because the rats are breaking out. Fucking poison rats ate the fucking baby. Why couldn't the fucking rat eat the baby? Then the fucking baby wouldn't turn me in."

"I know, Maggie. I know," said Adam. He let the weak flesh drape herself on him. He once viewed her at bus stops asking for money. The holy fools that spared their change received more affection from Maggie than they wanted. One penitent made the mistake of not pulling away from her when she hugged him and kissed him and got a full tongue kiss while she tried undoing his belt. He pushed her and she lay upon the sidewalk in the sidewalk. Adam was hiding in the shadows laughing.

Maggie was muttering in French. They walked into the intersection and Adam memorized the license numbers and letters. The price of the kiwi fruit wasn't significant; three days ago beat a tom tom sound in his head.

Listen, you fallen angels. Listen, mechanized joy. Hear, you fools. Love the silence; the silence in the numbers focused the devils of spirit in the unchanging nature of coffee. Faith and doctrine is water. Pass it off from a cloud and walk in cherry groves. Ted Kennedy bounces in the small trampolines. The formula of the world is chaos squared to regimentation over x times pi. X equals neshama to the infinite power. Philistines always insert McDonalds into x. You will fall but I can teach you the meaning of you.

Maggie bestowed her bony green arm upon his shoulder, Adam felt like a ventriloquist and wondered if she was his ventriloquist. Maybe he was really talking about his traitor son. Maybe she was betraying the illuminated dancers.

The clouds held the sky and Adam accepted the deluge. Her hands were sliding off his coat. He didn't want to know the reason. When they found a corner, they saw beautiful. A blue house confronted the corner, broken fence and roses sanctifying the window.

"What does it say, fucker?" said Maggie.

Adam didn't speak. He was waiting for the divine. Maggie was testing his faith.

"Fucker! What does the sign say?"

"This property condemned by the City. No trespassing."

Adam didn't see a bulldozer. Maggie was still clinging when he went down to supplicate. If he could smell the grass, he would have smelled jasmine, enough to whelm the sweat and shit clinging to his trousers.

"Fuck," said Maggie.

"It's in here," he said, "because you have to believe in this place, in the palace of the Ascension; Jesus can't hurt me. I know I have not been your most faithful servant. I should have let you; let your words heal but the agents corrupted my snow white innocence.

In the mountains of the gods, angels don't care. They will not interfere. You just sing mystic spheres as fascists rule material happiness. Everything fell apart in Dallas. They are not responsible. The mountains have stopped floating. Adam and Maggie approached the interior before Maggie offered a prayer of fuckery. Adam only heard the word.

Adam sought light switches to no avail. Maggie was laughing. All dry walls had been gutted. Stray wires and cables slithered from the hidden spaces. Blasphemers had rummaged through the house for copper. The mafia and the government agents had left their blue and green steps behind. He remembered the unconsecrated whiskey. His brain couldn't see the rats. They would never forgive. If the *Good Housekeeping* magazines had remembered, he would read them. A large 70s style television set served as the altar upon which all fearful trembling sacrifices could lay their burden.

Maggie was still praying; he didn't think she could see the television's message without electricity; the television blessed him with imagination. Every channel imparted the beatific Bob Barker. Simple fat pilgrims were bidding on washers, dryers and enlightenment. Enlightenment was cheaper than turtle wax. The top of JFK's skull was no longer a collector's item. A man with a pudgy face, a blue polo shirt and a walrus mustache adherent bid $399. That was an overbid. Prophecy went for $568. Adam had not readied himself to see Bob Barker's face.

"Remember to spay and neuter your monks," he said. Abelard wept.

"Have you found the bird yet?" asked Maggie.

"No."

"We need fucking turtle doves to satisfy your fucking mountain."

Was she really speaking? Adam didn't know. They brought him to the secret rooms and tried to talk. They told him to take their cancer pills.

"Goodnight, Maggie," said Adam.

"Go fuck yourself," said Maggie.

Adam stroked her hair with dry unworthy fingers. She didn't

believe him about the conspiracy. He knew she would never try to talk him away from his faith. She could be a good soldier. He ignored her small convulsions. She was cold before he removed his hand. She smelled like a tabby cat that had napped in his backyard when he was five, the one with the funny neck.

Adam stayed by her body until hunger forced him away. He walked into the world returned to the innocence of birth. He forgot about the mountains of the gods, after a memory.

CAMELOT, MARINER YEAR 1962

by John Grey

Jack Ruby spoke into his headset and his men listened. They were the best agents at the MIA and were spread throughout the parade route and scattered among many of the surrounding buildings. That entire section of Eisenhower City was a temporary no-fly zone. Security-wise, there was nothing more that he could do. When he wasn't whispering orders into five hundred ear-pieces, he was cursing the president under his breath.

"What's with that damn fool riding in an open vehicle? He can see just as well with shields and the crowds can see him. But Oswald wants to slap a few hands on the way. Really be in touch with his supporters. Don't blame me if something bad happens to the guy."

He laughed to himself. And then repeated with a sneer. "Yeah, don't blame me, Oswald."

The crank caller databases in Ruby's hand-pad were bursting at the seams. But those losers weren't the ones that bothered him. The real assassins didn't advertise. And they could strike from anywhere. Sure, Oswald was popular on Mariner (he won 70 percent of the vote in the last election) but, throughout the universe, it was a different story. Oswald's war machine didn't play well on the much-battered likes of Zordak and Gancher. And among that 30 percent on his home planet were those with some long held and deadly grudges.

The parade had already begun.

"Zapruder, how do we look?"

"We're passing Castro Plaza," he reported. "Crowds are going absolutely wild. They sure do love this guy. No sign of any trouble."

"Fine. Fine."

Ruby's number two man Zapruder rode shotgun in the car following the president. In his hand was a tiny remote that could activate the protective shields on the president's vehicle at any time. These were the latest technology—Super Safeguard. Men in the field called them Back-at-yer Glass.

"I know the Kennedys are here somewhere," Ruby muttered to himself. "This is just the opportunity they'd be looking for—Lee Oswald out of his fortress, bathing in the glory of victory over the Veranians."

For the past month, the television channels had been full of decimated Veranian cities and brave Marinerian soldiers.

"No one dare threaten us now," Oswald had announced with just obvious pride on his weekly broadcast to the planet.

But not everyone on Mariner was as obsessed with constant warfare as Oswald and his followers. But, judging by the last election, 70 percent were. The Kennedys operated on behalf of the other 30 percent. And the scattered survivors of races on all these so-called enemy planets.

Despite the best efforts of the MIA, Dick Nixon's men had never been able to uncover the Kennedy compound. Jack Ruby had twice been assigned to just such a mission and twice that mission had failed. The layers of lies and subterfuge were just too many and too impenetrable. The best shot at busting up the clan was an occasion like this—a regal procession in honor of the man they hated. Oswald was out in the open and now, with any luck, they would be, too.

Old Joe Kennedy was dead. That much was certain. His eldest son and namesake had been killed in the first Zordak War. Joe had been an Oswald supporter up until then. There was even talk of a vice-presidency for him. But the senseless death of his pride and joy changed all that. Up until then, wars were nothing to Old Joe but variations of the computer games he played as a boy. Killings were racked up like points and it was always the other guy getting blasted. Sure, these skirmishes could be taxing on the treasury but ultimately, the populace bathed in the glory of victory. And the exaltation, the exhilaration, spurred them to work harder. Any shortfalls in the budget were soon made up by greater output. The spoils of war, such as access to the Zordak mines, just made these excursions all the more appetizing.

But, in the Battle of the Roosevelt Belt, young Joe's vessel had been shot down by the supposedly much inferior weapons of a guerrilla Zordak vessel. Old Joe's heart was broken. Oswald referred to it as a win-win situation. "An easy victory, some glory for your boy," were his exact words. Old Joe had been lied to and his family and its brightest light had been extinguished. He turned on Oswald, even attempted an assassination of the president in the pentagonal office. But his Blazer misfired, Oswald engaged a desk shield, and Joe Kennedy exited the Red House before the MIA could respond, gathered up his family, and disappeared.

'They're here," Ruby muttered to himself. 'They've got to be in this crowd somewhere. They can disguise themselves all they want. But just let one of them open his mouth near me. I'd know those damn la-di-da Kennedy tonsils anywhere."

He was standing outside the Khrushchev building on Freedom Drive. Based on the information Zapruder was feeding, the president's heli-car would pass by him in another five minutes. He could hear cheers in the distance.

"Be alert," he repeated to all his men. "Be alert."

But there was a smirk that Ruby's serious façade could not quite erase. In truth, the Kennedys did not bother him. He had a man in their camp. Reports had been sporadic from his mole but if there was one constant in all the missives he'd been receiving since the Oswald love-fest was announced, it was the letter K. And, based on the parade route, that K could only mean one thing—the Khrushchev building.

He had his agents in the building. Not many but he figured the fewer the better. For he had his own plans.

High up in the Khrushchev building, the janitors were hard at work cleaning the office of Seabed Agriculture. The staff of the various companies and government agencies that occupied the twenty six floors were, almost to a man and woman, parked against windows that looked down on Freedom Drive. The excitement from the ground floor to the top was palpable. Only the two men running supra-chutes over various carpets on twenty six seemed immune to the Lee Harvey Oswald fever.

Occasionally, the two met up mid-floor for a whispered exchange. No one paid them any attention.

"So faw so good, Bobby."

"Right, Jack."

"Just got the wahhd from Sirhan. Interstellar Trade folks are all heading in this direction. Need to pay their respects to that pahhs of shit. Don't get me stahhdid on Oswald. Time to make our move."

The two janitors picked up their equipment, departed the room, strolled nonchalantly down the hall to the Interstellar Trade headquarters. They were greeted by the third of the trio, a very nervous looking Sirhan Sirhan.

"It's okay, Sirhan." Bobby tried to calm him down. "Everything's under control. We'll be done and out of here in no time. Just remember…we need you." He wrapped an arm around his shaking colleague.

"I just checked with Teddy on the roof, Bobby. Everything's in order. Once I give him the wahhd, he'll have MK here in a flahhsh."

"Sirhan's on edge. Maybe we should have used Lawford."

"That playboy. No way."

The view from Interstellar Trade was nowhere as close as that from the prime viewing spot in Seabed. But that didn't matter. They could still get a clear shot at the motorcade. And the office was adjacent to the staircase to the roof. Bobby began drilling tiny holes in the large windows that fronted Freedom Drive. Jack dismantled his and Bobby's supra-chutes and reassembled them into the latest in Blazers.

"Gawd bless MIT," declared Jack as he kissed his weapon. "Mariner Institute of Technology. The assassin's best friend."

Bobby laughed. Sirhan giggled nervously. He began breaking down his own supra-chute. His weapon was different, designed for short range. Sirhan's job was to watch the door and make sure there were no unwelcome visitors.

Jack and Bobby lined up their powerful weapons.

"I just hope Oswald doesn't change his mind and leave the shields up," remarked Bobby.

"That could get mahhhsy."

Even from their far away vantage point, they could still hear the cheers growing louder and louder. Jack's aim was steady. With the death of his older brother, he was his father's shining hope. His hatred of Oswald was more than an inheritance. The Kennedys had traveled widely, stuck together. They'd been to Zordak and Gancher, witnessed the wholesale destruction caused by Marinerian missiles: men and women, nothing but heads and torsos; little children with no arms. And for what—some imagined threat dreamed up by Oswald and his cronies, Howard Hunt, Sam Giacana and Lyndon Johnson. Give 'em wars and they'll vote for you. That was their motto. Just make sure they're conflicts they can end quickly with minimal losses on the Mariner side. Too bad if Joe Kennedy junior was one of those minimal losses.

Jack was charismatic, well spoken, despite his strange way with vowels and ending words with a renegade letter 'r'. People listened to him. Not just the professional disgruntled but former followers of Oswald with access to the inner chambers. And, with his boyish but handsome looks, women were drawn to him. There was glamorous Jackie…and sexy Marilyn…to name just two. Then there were the likes of Sirhan Sirhan. No one seems to remember who recruited him or when. Maybe it was Teddy. The younger brother was always bringing home stray sheep. And Sirhan was certainly that. To the Kennedys, he just seemed like a confused kid. Certainly apolitical. But he had nerve. And he was like a faithful lapdog. He had begged to be part of the mission. But Bobby couldn't help wondering why he seemed so anxious all of a sudden, why, as he and his brother steadied their aims, he could hear Sirhan's uneasy pacing in the background.

Ruby was ready. He knew the risk he was taking. But he no longer cared. Every so often he coughed just to remind himself of the cancer eating away at his lungs, courtesy of a stint at one of

Oswald's 'safe as houses' weapon testing sites. He'd been rewarded with a position high up in the ranks of the MIA, reporting directly to Nixon.

But what did that matter now. What did anything matter.

In the distance, he could see the Oswald vehicle approaching. Trailing it was Zapruder. "Typical of the man," thought Ruby. "He's fiddling with his watch camera. Why did I ever pick him for my second in command?"

Ruby continued to voice encouragement to all of his men whether on the sidewalks, in the buildings or on many of the rooftops. He had nobody however atop the Khrushchev tower. He couldn't remember why he hadn't considered that option. Ruby had no doubt the Kennedys were in that building somewhere. That didn't bother him. There'd be no glory this day for those sons-of-bitches.

The heli-car came nearer and nearer. Ruby tensed up.

"Zapruder, stop fucking with that camera."

"Yes, boss. I've got the president's back, boss. Don't worry."

Suddenly Ruby got word from Hoffa high up in the Che condominiums across the street.

"I see something in the Khrushchev, sir. Top floor. Far window. I'm trying to get a closer look at it. Lots of glare. Hard to see. But they could be long-range Blazers."

It was just as he expected.

"Shields, Zapruder!" he shouted. "Shields!"

Zapruder grabbed at the remote, his wrist camera still rolling.

"Shields going up," he shouted to the president.

Oswald turned around. He was annoyed but also, for the moment, fearful that they must have spotted a potential sniper. He knew it was a decision Nixon's security team wouldn't take lightly. And he was more than aware he had enemies. He was enjoying immensely this up-close and touchy-feely session. But if his planned high-fiving with the faithful required a minor interruption, then so be it.

Shields zipped up and over the president's heli-car at the very moment Jack pulled the trigger. For Bobby, distracted from his own shot by his brother's triumphant "Yes!" it was as if time was slowing, almost in a freeze. He felt as if he could see the Blazer stream, one long taut line of invisible fire-power, dispensed from their hiding place way up on the top floor of the Khrushchev building and sent straight to that tiny vehicle in the street below. His nerves tensed ready for that subsequent celebratory release. He knew his brother. No way he'd miss.

But with a hiss and a thump, just as that Blazer streak was about to slam into the president's head, the shield zipped into place, thwacked the ray like a baseball bat, back in the direction from which it came. Bobby saw it all but could not get his words of warning out in time.

Jack turned toward his brother, to share their success, at the same moment as the window shattered, glass flew everywhere and Jack's own Blazer beam boomeranged into the back of his skull.

"No!" screamed Bobby.

He did not notice Sirhan with his gun raised and pointed toward him. Sirhan's first target had been Jack but his nerve froze as his finger fumbled for the trigger. His plan was to kill him at the moment Jack steadied and aimed his weapon. But his intended victim had fired that shot with Sirhan standing by uselessly. Bobby was a different story. He'd dropped his weapon. He was one minute weeping beside his brother's body, the next, fearful the MIA would be bursting into the room.

Down below, Ruby's men did not need instructions from their leader. They converged on the Khrushchev building. Those already inside were making a bee-line for the offices of Interstellar trade.

"What's going on?"

Bobby could hear Teddy's voice through his earpiece.

"Jack's been shot."

"Jesus. Let's get him out of there. I'll get MK now."

"No. Wait. It's no use. Jack's gone. I'm on my way.'

But as he turned to leave, Sirhan fired. His panicked shot blew Bobby's shoulder to pieces. He dropped.

"It's Sirhan…he's turned…" He dropped to the floor in agony. "Get out of there, Teddy. I'm done for. Go. Go."

Teddy did not wait to be told. With one word into his mouthpiece, their escape rocket would be on its way. He prayed that, with all the chaos below, it would elude the MIA's radar.

Sirhan stood over the fallen Bobby, fired a second round, this time right into his chest.

Ruby rushed to the president's car. In the background, he could hear Zapruder screaming out, "I've got it all on view! Wahoo! Amazing!"

A medical team followed Ruby. Nearby agents stepped aside for their leader. Ruby gestured to Zapruder to lift the shields.

"Are you okay, mister president?" asked one of the doctors.

"Yes," he insisted. "I'm fine. It's those damn Kennedys. I know it is."

"Don't worry about the Kennedys, sir," said Ruby. "We have that situation well in hand."

One medical man ran a scan over Oswald's chest, another did the same for his brain. Jack Ruby let out a loud cough that distracted the president from the doctors.

"You should do something about that cough," Oswald advised Ruby.

"Yes," he replied. "I think I will. Right now as a matter of fact."

Ruby pulled out his weapon, pointed it at Oswald, screamed, "Take this, you bay of pigs!" and plugged him twice in the chest.

The crowd surrounding the president was in total shock. Both medical men toppled backward from the impact to the body, their faces and hands splattered with blood. It took three of Ruby's own men, trained to react to such scenarios, to grab their leader by the arms, disarm and cuff him. But Jack Ruby had no wish to run. The president's assassin smiled and went quietly.

Zapruder watched, in disbelief, as his boss was led away. He was now in charge. That took a few minutes to sink in as well. He squeezed through the mob, many of whom were already wailing in sorrow, caught up with the three MIA agents as they were shoving Ruby into an unmarked heli-car that had been parked down a side street. Zapruder grabbed his former boss's head set and began chirping orders.

"Some kind of sun-jet on the top of the Khrushchev building," a voice screamed into his ear piece.

"Don't let it get away," Zapruder fired back.

But it was too late. As agents headed up to the roof, Mary Jo had already hovered into place, thrown down a ladder and Ted had scrambled up into the cockpit of the sun-jet and was speeding away, out of the city and across the Chappaquiddick Ocean.

"I'll take the wheel," Ted said.

"Are you sure you're okay?"

"No, I'm not okay. Jack dead. Bobby dead. It's like our family's under some kind of curse. I just want to get the hell out of here."

The first agent to the roof could see the sun-jet gathering speed. It would be beyond his range in a matter of seconds. He fired his Blazer at the retreating vehicle but the heli-jet was out of sight in an instant and there was no way of telling if he'd hit anything.

But Mary Jo heard a crack at the rear of the vehicle.

"What was that?" Teddy asked.

He was buckled in, at the controls and swinging the vehicle wide, scattering radar baffles in all directions so his course couldn't be tracked.

"Looks like we've been hit," exclaimed Mary Jo. "Not too bad."

"Steering's not good," Teddy said frantically. "We're losing altitude. Don't think she'll make it back to the compound. I'm heading for the Vineyard Isles."

"Okay."

She huddled close to Ted as he struggled to control the vehicle. It swerved from side to side and continued to drop.

"The isles are ahead!" he shouted. "We should make it!"

Mary Jo checked the landing gear. It was out of commission. There was no way he could bring it down on land. He'd have to do one very risky swan-dive into the ocean. There was barely time for breath. Waves loomed up, like frantic hands grabbing at the sun-jet.

"Brace yourself," he told her.

She grabbed the sides of her pilot seat, squeezed up everything from legs to eyes. The vehicle smacked a breaker, was sprayed violently and then its nose dipped, cut into the water. One wing snapped. The other rose up and rolled them over. Teddy pressed the button to retract the roof. He unbuckled and flung himself upward. Mary Jo tried to follow but was not as quick to release her belt or as certain a swimmer. The waves flung her backward. She screamed as the sun-jet buckled, squeezed down on her flailing body and, with Mary Jo gasping for air, sunk all the way to the bottom of the ocean.

Ted, operating on the same adrenaline that had brought the plane down, pitched himself at the first wave. It picked him up, tossed him forward, threw him like a beach ball before his arms and feet became fully engaged and he swam arduously toward shore.

From time to time, he looked behind him to see if Mary Jo was following but there was no sign of her or the sun-jet. By the time he scrambled up to the beach and flopped his weary body on the sand, it was clear to his breaking heart that he was the only survivor of the mission.

He struggled to his feet, looked up at the distant retreating sun and screamed.

THE CUBAN EXILE CRISIS

by Tony Laplume

Joan Kennedy had been attempting to live her life as anonymously as possible. Part of this was made possible by the particular rules of her current residence, the Republic of Cuba, which had taken to isolationism in recent decades. By the rules of Cuban citizenship, she was not allowed to leave the country for any reason. When the invasion of the Danab struck Earth, she wondered if any complications would ensue, since she came from a family that might have been expected to take a leading interest in preserving humanity's future.

There was also the small matter of the curse to consider. It wasn't a curse, exactly, perhaps only the perception of one. Members of her family didn't tend to fare well when they stuck their necks out. Joan was not in any way a notable member of the family, either by her own activities or through immediate relations, but she was always aware that this probably wouldn't matter when the chips were down. She wasn't one to take risks, Kennedy or not.

She had caught a lot of grief, making the decision to live in Cuba. Everyone Joan knew thought it was a bad idea, and they weren't afraid to tell her. It got to the point where perfect strangers offered their opinion unsolicited, somehow recognizing her, even when she wore that ridiculous wig and shades. Come to think of it, Joan had been told once or twice that it made her resemble one of her ancestors. She tended to ignore these things until it got her in trouble. That was the running theme of Joan's life, "until it got her in trouble." She failed to learn this distinction with considerable glee.

In Cuba there were plenty of distractions, but Joan preferred the music. She didn't have much to do otherwise, so she would park herself in front of any given performer, completely careless of the potential danger, and listen, right in the middle of the street sometimes. Joan made several good friends that way, people she brought into her home, even if they said they wouldn't play any more music. She would offer them a drink, and hope that they had things to say. Joan was more of a listener than a talker. Whenever she spoke, it was invariably about the family, and not by choice.

That was its own kind of curse.

When the war for mankind became unavoidable, when Cuba could no longer pretend that it existed in a vacuum, Joan struggled with what she would do. Every Cuban faced this dilemma, but for Joan personally she remembered all over again her distinguished ancestors, whom she could never escape, and wondered what they would do. She had no family here, and for the first time became keenly aware that the family had always relied on its own support to make decisions like this. The government prepared its defenses but otherwise held firm that none of its people, natural or otherwise, would cross its borders to fight elsewhere.

The news remained grim. Thousands died every day. The Danab were relentless. Joan kept waiting for heroes to emerge. Although she didn't feel like she could be one herself, it was always at the back of her mind that she might be forced into the role. She turned to her cat for solace. Bobbi's ears were unique for the feline kind. They were always flipped back. For any other cat, the ears would flap back up, but not Bobbi's. It made her distinguished, or so Joan liked to think. Like any cat owner, Joan tended to take any and every sign that her cat was unique and special. For Joan, Bobbi's unique physical distinction was almost enough to make it an honorary Kennedy.

"I should probably break the rule," she said to her cat. "It's the right thing to do. It's what people would expect of me. Sometimes expectations have to be met. Sometimes expectations are important. What do you think?"

The cat stared briefly into Joan's eyes, and then shook its head. The ears remained flipped back.

"If I stay, I may very well die anonymously," she continued the nonexistent conversation. "If I go, I could die gloriously, probably horribly, but gloriously. My whole family is probably working on this problem. We should probably sit tight for now, shouldn't we?"

If they were, they'd been considering it for the past few years. Joan stayed in contact with her parents, but communications had been terrible for months now. She hadn't had a decent conversation in weeks. Somehow she never talked about what she should do. The cat licked its paw, preparing to groom. Joan watched for a few moments and tried to concentrate. She should fight. She *had* to fight. It would be beyond selfish to watch the end of the world from Cuba, even if it would be an irony.

The patrols had increased. Her home was watched just as much as everyone else's, but Joan was a keen observer, mostly because she watched more than participated in the world around her. She knew how to escape this curious prison. She certainly had connections. Getting out of Cuba wouldn't be the problem. It was what would follow, not just the war with the menacing alien Danab, but the Cuban government's reaction once it realized she was missing. They wouldn't just let her disappear. They would track her down. That's the way Cuba was these days.

If Joan had one advantage, it was that she knew exactly who they would send. It would be Ishida. He was their answer to everything and had been assigned to monitor Joan since her arrival.

It was midnight when she began her escape, but the sky was alight with explosions like it had been for years. Sometimes Joan could hear the explosions. Sometimes it was only the eerie silence. Putting Bobbi into a carrying case, she made her way down to the harbor, where a network of acquaintances had arranged her passage aboard one of the frequent cargo vessels Cuba invariably turned away from its ports. There were familiar faces aboard, American, yet Joan found herself cloaked in anonymity. These days, people had other things on their mind. She quickly located a berth in the lower decks and settled in for the journey homeward.

Days later, Joan was wandering the ship when she became aware that someone was watching her. She looked all around but could find no one looking, certainly not at her, even if they were being discreet about it. It had to be Ishida. Wherever he was, he had finally revealed himself. He was playing his usual game. He would let her do most of the work herself. The closer they reached her destination, the more aware she'd become of the inevitable. Ishida would not allow her to step foot in another country.

Joan could approach the captain and request asylum, protection, but that would only draw attention to her. She was in a precarious situation. Ishida wouldn't stop until he'd achieved his goal, and he wouldn't much care who got in his way. He had diplomatic immunity, so even if he murdered her in front of everyone he couldn't be touched and Cuba would never prosecute him.

Her advantage was that Joan knew Ishida's basic character. The one weakness in the Cuban agent's arsenal was that he liked a pretty face. Joan was pretty sure that this had been the reason why he'd chosen her as an assignment in the first place. He was fascinated by her eyes. Usually people paid attention to a Kennedy face for almost anything else, but Ishida seemed to have figured out that the unifying element was the eyes. Joan tried to figure out what the fascination was all about, and all she could decide was that they were the only feature that anyone could have asserted as grounding her in a more serious light. They looked old to her, serious. She hated them.

She decided that she wouldn't allow Ishida to intimidate her. Out in the open Joan could hide in plain sight, limit the agent's movements. For once she could embrace her own latent celebrity. The effect was immediate. She was no longer a Cuban. No one aboard this ship even thought of her this way, and perhaps most of them didn't even know, only some regular readers of the tabloids, where Joan's mild exploits in Havana were typically exaggerated. She made an effort to draw attention to herself, acted the part of the spoiled débutante. Everyone wanted a piece of her. It was like the old days, what she had tried to escape. She fought the anxiety that rose up from the pit of her stomach, a small price to pay if there was even the slightest chance that she could hope to evade Ishida. Just along the edge of the mounting crowd she saw him, cool and collected as always. All this excitement, however, would further befuddle him, his obsession.

Someone broke the spell in a few moments, though, a misanthrope. "Why are you making such a fuss over this girl? The whole world's collapsing around us and you're acting like the world pivots around her!"

The mood changed in an instant. Joan's fellow passengers, the legal ones unlike herself, began to disperse. Ishida waited patiently. The misanthrope was right, of course, but Joan wondered if there was so much harm in giving people a respite from the apocalypse, the alien invasion that had been prophesied for years and finally come. If there was anything incongruous about this moment, it was that Ishida was spending his time tracking her down, after all a completely meaningless woman, instead of fighting to preserve the future of humanity. Selfish thought, but she wondered if it had even occurred to Ishida.

She watched as he made his approach. As always, his eyes were locked on hers, and she wasn't sure if he was looking at her or indulging his fancy. "You made it pretty far," Ishida said, no trace of emotion in his voice. "Not far enough."

"Story of my life," Joan said. "You can't blame a girl for trying."

"This was always the way it was going to end. You made your attempt. You knew it would fail. I'm only sorry that it had to be me who finished it."

"No, you're sorry that you fell in love with me."

"Perhaps."

The blade he produced was longer than she expected, something that must have been hidden behind Ishida's back, probably for as long as she'd known him. It shined in the sunlight, nearly blinding her. They were alone now, Joan Kennedy finally deserted, isolated. Her mother had always warned her about that. "Don't do it in public. Avoid the spectacle."

"I'm not a bad person," Joan said. "You know that. I'm only trying to do what's right."

"So am I."

"There's a difference and you know it. What you're about to do is murder. I'm trying to make a difference. That's all I want. All my life I've been hiding from it, pretending that I was anything but what I am, denying the legacy that was always there in front of me. I kept turning away. I thought I understood. I was an idiot. Just give me this chance. Let me go out on my own terms."

"You know that won't happen."

"It's a curse, then."

"Seems that way."

The blade was midway through her torso when Joan finally felt it. She looked into Ishida's eyes, saw nothing, saw everything. There were a million things she wanted to say, but couldn't find the words. It wasn't the fact that she was dying, but that she didn't think he would do it, not even the moment it happened. That was probably how it had happened each and every time. That was the real curse, the denial of reality, the inability to do anything but what had to be done. The news would be devastating to Cuba. She knew that, better than Ishida. She saw it in his eyes. He had never even considered what his actions would mean to him, how it put an end to his story, too. Her death would be a rallying point. Her life would mean something after all.

In her last moments, Joan decided she was okay with that.

THE COST
OF FREEDOM

by Milo James Fowler

"Things do not happen. Things are made to happen."
– John F. Kennedy

The Klaggsron wasn't buying any of it.

"You have interfered in our affairs for the last time, Human," the translator box, strapped to its flabby mottled throat, grated out in a mechanical monotone.

Jack faced the hideous creature across the Oval Office. He'd made it clear to his staff in no uncertain terms that the two of them were to be undisturbed.

"It was never our intention to overstep, Ambassador. You must understand, things on Earth are not as you might expect. Unlike your world, here our peoples coexist—"

"There is always a slave race and a master race. Such is the way of the universe. You will not be allowed to give the Greys freedom they do not deserve. They are parasites. Bottom-feeders."

Jack narrowed his gaze. The White House facilities crew wouldn't appreciate the Klaggsron's acid sweat dripping onto the carpet, sizzling as it burned the edges of the presidential seal.

"Ambassador, I must humbly remind you: my planet, my rules. Everyone has the God-given right to be free."

The Klaggsron's bulbous trio of eyeballs twitched, pulsating with consternation, yet its tone through the translator remained unchanged. "Who are you to undermine galactic policy? The Greys are a subspecies—they have no discernible rights."

"Here, they do." Jack nodded politely as he stepped behind his desk. "Now if you'll excuse me, I have to plan a trip to Texas. And believe me when I say it's the last place on Earth I'd rather visit." He chuckled amiably.

The Klaggsron lashed out with a poison-tipped tentacle that spooled from one of the orifices gaping across its emaciated midsection. "Allow me to save you the trouble, Human."

Jack had half-expected as much. He turned quickly and jerked back at the waist, dodging the lethal projectile, at the same time tugging open his desk drawer and grabbing the first thing in sight: a gleaming incinerator pistol.

The Klaggsron's eyes nearly popped from their sockets. "Damn you, Jack Kennedy," its translator box droned.

"Likewise." Jack pulled the trigger, and the Ambassador dematerialized with a puff of white smoke—not unlike something from a B-movie at the Saturday matinee.

A knock sounded at the door. Not the secret service; they knew better. It had to be—

"Come in, LB." Jack returned the incinerator to its drawer and admired the pistol's chrome-like alloy, the sensual curve of the cylinder, how it seamlessly merged with the barrel. He'd fired it once or twice before, and each time it surprised him how much devastating power could be contained by such a gorgeous weapon.

The door burst open, and in stomped the vice president, sputtering curses in his southern drawl and waving away the dissipating cloud in the center of the room. "Don't you even bother tryin' to explain this one, Jack."

"Self-defense." Jack closed the drawer and leaned forward with his palms on the desktop. "You know how they can be."

"The Klaggsrons aren't my concern, Mr. President. It's the humans 'round here that bother me. The little ones, in particular." He half-turned to glare at the serviceman reaching in to shut the door behind him. "What the hell are you lookin' at, son?"

"Mr. Johnson hasn't had his coffee yet." Jack winked at the serviceman, who ducked his head and disappeared as the door closed.

"Don't even drink the damn stuff." LB started pacing, hands

folded behind his back in a pose that would have been awkward for a human. "What was I saying?"

"Little ones."

"Right. The ones that like to crawl around under that big desk of yours. What's to keep 'em from finding all those alien gadgets you've got stashed away?"

"Lock," Jack said. Instantly, the drawer in the Resolute desk containing the incinerator pistol clicked. "I don't think we need to worry about John-John overriding my voice commands, LB. Not until his voice changes, at any rate."

Johnson threw up his hands. "It's your funeral—or your son's." He blew out a sigh, his wrinkled cheeks undulating. "Fate has a way of catching up with us, Jack. You can't keep throwing your weight around with those damned alien freaks and think it won't come back to bite you on the ass."

Jack nodded, frowning at the Klaggsron residue on the carpet as he came around to the front of his desk. He folded his arms, creasing the pressed navy blue suit. "You don't have to remind me. I know what lies ahead."

LB's mechanical eyes narrowed. He appraised the President for a moment. "It's a heavy burden—"

"But it's mine to bear." Jack leaned back against his desk. "Mine alone."

"Your curse, I suppose. The most powerful man in the free world—not to mention this end of the galaxy." LB's head pivoted side to side on silent hydraulics. "About to give his life for a bunch of *greybacks*."

Jack sniffed at the derogatory term. LB hadn't lost any of his southern charms after the transfer of his conscious self into the mechanized clone. This cyborg was more than just a ghost inside a machine.

"What do we know about the chameleon?"

"Only that he's in Texas," Jack said. They had a Grey informant tailing him. No one really knew what the chameleons were—whether an alien race unto themselves or some bizarre kind of alien-human hybrid. Regardless, they were form-changers, and the Greys were concerned by their presence on Earth. And if they were concerned,

Jack was concerned. "He'll make his play while I'm there."

"So says your almighty oracle?" LB chuckled with obvious disdain. "We got any ID on 'im?"

"Oswald. Lee Harvey. Works at a book depository."

"Sounds as all-American as they come." LB cleared his throat—a pointless gesture, but a very human one. Some biological remnants remained for the sake of appearances. Anthropomorphic machines made some Americans nervous, after all. "It's not too late, Jack. You don't have to go through with this." He strode forward a step and halted. "Think of tonight as your Gethsemane. But you can most definitely let your cup pass."

"Careful." Jack winked at his second-in-command. "We've got enough on our hands already. Don't you dare add blasphemy to the list."

LB cursed with a smirk. "Why not just let the greybacks fight their own battles?"

Jack shook his head at the cyborg with the face of an old codger. "You forget, LB. It's our battle as much as theirs. We have a proud history of throwing off the shackles of tyranny—first the British, then slavery in the South, then the Soviets with their plague of red states spreading across the globe. We did what no other nation on the earth could do. We provided a home for an alien race with nowhere else to go. We are a nation of immigrants, LB. And our Grey brothers and sisters have come here from a distant star to find peace. I will not have them routed out by the very tyrants they sought to escape from, across light years, time and space. The Klaggsrons will not succeed, no matter how many *ambassadors* they teleport into this very office."

LB squinted up one eye. "Nice speech, Mr. President. But who the hell's going to keep killing them off after you're gone?"

Jack gave the cyborg a sad attempt at a smile. "I'll leave you the incinerator in my will."

Marilyn came calling late that night.

Jackie and the kids had already turned in, Jackie needing her beauty sleep before the big day tomorrow, and the kids needing both members of the first couple to kiss them goodnight before they could fall asleep. Jackie took it a step further, of course, telling John Jr. and Caroline each a different homemade bedtime story while Jack stood in the doorway and listened with half a smile at the perfection of it all. The media had it right: Jackie was an angel.

But for a man like Jack, her weight on one shoulder left him lopsided. He had to balance things out.

So there was Marilyn. A devil in a white dress, escorted into the Oval Office in the dead of night by the same mum secret serviceman who'd shut the door on the irate vice president earlier. The same serviceman who'd seen to the carpet cleaning, assigning a White House facilities crew who'd become experts at removing alien droppings from the hallowed carpet.

"Oh, Jack." She fell into his arms as soon as the door closed, after the President gave the verbal command to lock out any potential intruders—little ones in search of Daddy after a bad dream, in particular.

"You've been drinking again." He appreciated the pressure of her supple curves against him for only a moment before letting her down into an armchair. "I thought we agreed you'd lay off the stuff. It makes you—"

"Fuzzy, yeah, I know." She giggled, reaching for his crotch with a playful squeeze.

"Marilyn." He took her chin in his hand. "I need you to see."

"Oh, I'm seeing fine. The Kennedy monument is *fully*—"

His gripped her cheeks. Playtime was over. "I need you to *see*."

She dropped her hands into the lap of her white sequined dress, form-fitting, voluptuous. Any other time, any other place, it wouldn't have stayed on her for very long. But this was the Oval Office, and LB had his mechanical minions all over the White House plugged in and recording everything they could get their paranoid robotic eyes on. Jack let the vice president think it was a well-kept secret; he didn't really mind being spied on by the cyborg. He had nothing to hide—most of the time. And it was all in the interests of national security.

Jackie turned a blind eye to Jack's extracurricular activities, choosing not to see what others might; but she wouldn't be able to deny full-framed footage of Marilyn on her back atop the Resolute desk, should LB decide to share such a thing with her. That just wouldn't do at all.

"I can't, Jack." She wouldn't meet his gaze.

"You did last time."

"That was before—"

He squeezed her face almost hard enough to leave bruises on either side of her mouth, those luscious lips. Her eyes flashed up at him.

"Before I knew, damn it!" She slapped his hand away and collapsed back into the chair, slouching with her knees together and her shapely legs angled out. "You can't make me see that again, see what happened—what's going to happen to you. You can't, Jack. I won't!"

He rested his hand on her bare shoulder, the skin softer than anything he'd ever imagined before meeting her. There was something special about Marilyn, and it wasn't just her ability to see what nobody else could. "It's one possible future. That's all. Nobody's fate is set in stone."

Her eyes welled with tears. The mascara started to ooze. "But it's the same every time I look, Jack." She lurched forward to clutch his hand in both of hers. "You're in that limousine, and there's a shot, and Jackie, she goes after it, the back—not even a moment's pause— no hysterics at all. That wouldn't be me. If I saw you—"

"Lose my head?" He winked down at her.

"That's not funny."

He pressed her hand. "I just need to know where the shot's fired. I need to see his face."

"The shooter? How am I supposed to see that? I've only got eyes for you." The playful demeanor returned in an instant. She licked her lips and batted her long eyelashes up at him.

"You gave us a name last time: Oswald. The Greys say he's a chameleon—"

"You're gonna get shot by an *alien*? How's that make any sense? You're the one standing up for their rights!"

Jack shook his head, focusing on the moment. He didn't have much time. Air Force One went wheels up in the morning, and he and Jackie would be taking a direct flight to Texas. "Just one more time. That's all I'm asking."

"That's what I thought you'd say, Jack." She bit her lip and wiped at her eyes. "But I thought we'd be doing something a whole lot funner."

"That's not a word." He winked at her.

"It will be. Someday." Marilyn's eyes went white—not by rolling up into their sockets. The iris and pupil had vanished into a preternatural fog, and now she stared straight ahead as if seeing into another world.

"That's my girl." Jack sank to one knee beside her, holding her hand tight. "Tell me what you see."

It was no secret the Johnson and Kennedy clans despised each other. The two families were almost as different as humans and Greys. When the first alien ship crashed in Roswell twenty years ago, the Johnsons had been like Southern royalty, and LB was on the cutting edge of robotics, testing all manner of artificial limbs on veterans from the war. After the Greys arrived seeking refuge and offering the technology they'd stolen from the Klaggsrons— nanotech, biofuels, cybernetics—in exchange for a safe haven, the Johnsons jumped at the chance, taking the definition of cyborg to a whole new level. As a result, LB and Ladybird were barely human anymore, and they would live longer than anyone else on the planet.

"Trouble sleeping?" Jack spoke up once he'd reached the bottom of the basement stairs.

LB didn't bother to glance back at him. "Took the words right out of my mouth." They both knew he was the one who never slept.

Jack surveyed the laboratory—deep in the bowels under the White House—with as much interest as he could muster. Hands in the pockets of his navy blue slacks, he came up alongside LB who was, by all appearances, completely immersed in his latest project: a full-size incubation chamber capable of bringing an adult clone to term.

"Will it be ready in time?"

"What did that slut tell you?"

"Watch your mouth, LB. It'll get you in trouble, one of these days."

The vice president smirked. "So she *can* see the future."

"Sometimes I really wish you had an off switch."

LB actually chuckled at that. "See for yourself." He gestured toward the clone, lying on its back like Frankenstein's monster. "It ain't easy building an Irish Catholic bag of crap from scratch, but I did my best."

"Bag of circuits, more like." Jack pressed on the clone's abdomen, as rigid as an overstuffed chair.

"Programmed to smile and wave. And all without the stench of those wetworks you carry around with you." LB shook his head. "Someday, in a brighter future, everybody will have their brains transferred into a machine like this, and the world will—"

"Glad I won't be around to see it."

"Pessimist." LB clucked his artificial tongue.

"Optimist—assuming everything goes according to plan."

"Did she see Oswald's face?"

"Better." Jack turned to leave the cyborg to his crowning achievement. "She saw your clone take a bullet to the head."

◊ ◊ ◊ ◊ ◊

Dark Side Station 1 didn't receive many calls from Earth. Jack could tell that much right away by the moronic look on the Soviet's face.

"Do you know who I am?" Jack held the translator box—one of the alien gadgets from his desk—to his throat as he faced the Vidscreen. His question came through loud and clear in the tongue of dear Mother Russia.

The Soviet's jerky black and white image nodded quickly. His eyes had yet to blink, and his mouth sagged open like an imbecile's.

"Then get your commandant on the line before I blow a new crater in that moon."

The scrawny Soviet scurried out of the camera's range, and moments later a hard-eyed man in uniform chewing a cigar stub appeared on the screen. Jack knew him by appearance and reputation; they'd met only once before in person prior to the Sputnik launch. His name was Perchik.

"Mr. President," Perchik muttered. "Shouldn't you be packing?"

"Killed my second Klaggsron this week."

"That must be some kind of record, eh?"

"If you can't keep a single Klaggsron from teleporting to Earth, what are you going to do when their armada arrives?"

Perchik wrinkled his nose in disdain. "We will be prepared. Do not worry."

"I'll be heading up to supervise your *preparations* myself—as soon as I take care of a few things in Dallas."

"Trouble on the home front, Mr. President?"

"Nothing I can't handle."

Though he had his doubts. The Democratic party was coming apart at the seams in Texas, with certain factions supporting the President's position on the Greys while others clamored for a Humans First candidate to represent their interests at the next convention. Then there were those who fervently supported LB running against Jack, since the President's sour relations with the mob were common knowledge and many in the South were in favor of a fully-evolved mechanical man running the country, one who would act logically, rationally, and who couldn't be bought. Thankfully, they were in the minority. But the strains on the party were still a clear and present danger.

"Leave a hanger bay open for me. I'll join you in twenty-four hours."

To most of the world, humankind had yet to set foot on the moon. But a joint US and Soviet station had already been built on the dark side that never faced Earth, outfitted with a forcefield projector intended to deflect any Klaggsron teleportations. It had its glitches, however, as was plain to see every time one of those ambassador/assassins showed up in the Oval Office. They would keep coming through until the Earth Shield was at full capacity.

Also unbeknown to most of the humans on planet Earth, the Klaggsron armada was six months away, according to the Greys' estimates. The only thing that would turn them back would be a fully functional Dark Side station. Already the shipyards were working around the lunar clock, churning out spaceworthy attack vessels to meet the Klaggsrons in battle as soon as they passed Pluto; but Jack and Krushchev both knew they'd be little more than cannon fodder, intended to slow down the alien fleet while Dark Side's defenses kicked in. Once they did, nobody would make it through to Earth.

There were as many US workers as Soviets as there were Greys on Dark Side Station 1; it was a joint effort, with each side gaining what they wanted most. For the Greys, freedom from oppression. For the Soviets, access to certain technology Jack allowed the Greys to pass on to them. For the US and Jack Kennedy, peace on earth— always a good thing to have on one's resume while heading into an election year.

"Very well. Get your house in order, Mr. President." Perchik sniffed indifferently. "We look forward to welcoming you to Dark Side 1."

There was just one more *T* to cross before the night was through.

"How the hell'd you get this number?" Hoffa growled on the other end of the line, sounding more Neanderthal than human.

"Same way those Klaggsrons keep slipping through White House security, Jimmy boy." Jack held the receiver to one ear and gazed out at the night lights of D.C. through his office window. "Glitches. But I don't have to tell you about that."

Hoffa growled curses under his breath. "Ain't my fault you invited the wrong little green men into your bed. You might be wanting to switch sides before the next election, Mr. President."

"I assume you know about my trip tomorrow."

"Your cowboy friends ain't too keen on your Grey-lovin' either, huh?"

"Word is there's a chameleon down there with the name Oswald. Friend of yours?"

Hoffa paused. "You got some real balls. No wonder the dames line up outside your bedroom door." He barked a cough. "I don't know what you're implying, but I don't like it. I run a clean organization here. *Humans First.* I don't do business with any of them alien freaks. That's your angle."

"So if you were planning to make a play against me in Dallas—"

"I'd send a pure-blooded American to knock your block off." The line clicked, followed by a dial tone.

"Goodnight, Jimmy." Jack absently set the receiver into its cradle.

Air Force One maintained an altitude of thirty thousand feet with little turbulence as it soared on a direct route to Fort Worth, Texas. Jack poured over his notes for the fifth time while Jackie dozed across the cabin. LB seated himself rigidly beside the President.

"All set?" Jack didn't bother to look up.

The cyborg nodded. "We'll make the switch prior to the motorcade. Assuming your Hollywood *bitch* is as all-seeing as you seem to think she is, the clone will take the bullet, and you'll be free to save the world."

That was the plan, anyway. Fake his death and head up to Dark Side 1 to oversee Earth's defenses against the Klaggsron armada. Only a few elite members of the US and Soviet governments knew that such space travel was possible, thanks to the Greys. They couldn't let the general public know about such a thing; where there was one chameleon, there could be more, and if they were agents of some unknown alien organization, then it was a matter of global security to keep such information secret at all costs. Jack couldn't have the Klaggsrons finding out about the Earth Shield; as far as they were concerned, Earth was a sitting duck.

"She's an oracle." Jack eyed the cyborg with a steely gaze. "You won't refer to her in any other way."

Marilyn's visions had shown the Texas School Book Depository, sixth floor, with the muzzle of an Italian-made rifle nudged out onto the windowsill. But no Oswald. No face to go with the precognition.

Who was he working for? It wasn't like the Klaggsrons to send someone else to do their dirty work. Had the Humans First organization hired him to take out the President? Unlikely—unless Oswald had infiltrated them as a human with legitimate mob ties and been given his marching orders from Hoffa himself. Or was it possible the chameleon was acting alone—a member of some subversive alien group affiliated with neither the mob nor the Klaggsrons?

LB smirked. "She's a train wreck waiting to happen. You're completely unaware of the effect you've had on her. The drugs, the booze—it's all because of you." LB shook his head with what could have almost been mistaken for concern. "You're too much for her."

Jack returned his attention to his notes. "Then it's a good thing I'm about to die."

◊ ◊ ◊ ◊ ◊

There's something about a US President visiting you in person. You tend to forget what minor squabbles were threatening to burst your political party's bubble. Suddenly you're all smiles and firm handshakes and offers of the finest brandy in plush receiving rooms of the most elegant hotels any southern state has to offer.

Or maybe that was just the effect Jack Kennedy had on his supporters—even those unhappy with his current policy on the alien situation.

His speech had been direct: the United States, of all the nations on Earth, had been chosen by the Greys as their last bastion. And in return for their hospitality, the US had received incredible advances in technology; in the coming months, Americans could look forward to automobiles that would run on agricultural fuel sources, portable phones they could carry on their persons, and computers that would sit on a desk instead of fill half a room. All because the US had decided to live up to its reputation, inscribed on the Statue of Liberty herself: *Give me your tired, your poor, your huddled masses yearning to breathe free.*

Jack had ended his speech by saying, "No matter what galaxy you're from, if freedom is what you seek, then you are welcome in the United States of America."

He could tell he hadn't won over the hard-liners of the Humans First persuasion, but he hadn't intended to. The majority of the audience had erupted in thunderous applause, and if that was any indication, he had the Texas Democratic Party back on his side.

If not, they soon would be. Of this, he had no doubt. Presidential assassinations tended to have that effect on a nation's people.

They would choose to overlook his faults and failures, and he would become a legend. What he stood for would become more important than the man himself, and somehow the two would become one. And the Greys would have a new champion: the American people themselves, determined to honor the President's legacy of offering freedom to every race and species in the galaxy.

That was the plan, anyway. Now Jack just had to see it through.

The sixteen cars in the President's motorcade gleamed under the warm Texas sun. People in droves had lined up along the sidewalks to catch a glimpse of the first couple in their convertible Lincoln Continental. Four Dallas motorcycle cops escorted the Kennedys, winding through the streets slowly, giving the first lady and her husband ample opportunity to smile and wave at all who had gathered. It was a moment like no other in the history of Dallas. Camelot had come to town.

Tugging the baseball cap low on his forehead, Jack stuffed his hands into the pockets of his work jacket and trotted up the stairs of the book depository. Three young blacks passed him on their way down, talking and laughing excitedly.

"You're goin' the wrong way, man!" They chuckled, the heels of their shoes clapping as they quickly descended the stairwell.

Jack felt a sudden twinge of emotion. In a few minutes, the lives of these young people and millions like them would never be the same. America would freeze in time, suspended in horror. How could a *nobody* slay a king?

But it had to be done. For the freedom of an alien race, and for the future of the planet.

Gripping the incinerator pistol in his left pocket, Jack forged ahead, determined to find the *nobody* who would make history.

The sixth floor was empty, the halls silent. Jack crept toward the southeast corner, walking heel to toe as fast as he could without making a sound. On the streets below, spectators noisily anticipated the arrival of the presidential motorcade, still five minutes out.

Jack arrived at a storage room overlooking the street. Boxes of books stood in stacks on either side of a window with a clear view. A Mannlicher-Carcano rifle lay across two cardboard boxes, situated next to the windowsill. Beside the weapon stood an undersized man with his arms crossed, staring outside transfixed, as if he were already frozen in time.

"Hello, Oswald."

The man pivoted, in a single movement snatching the rifle and chambering a round, stock held firmly against his shoulder. He obviously knew his way around human weapons.

But Jack was well-acquainted with his incinerator. He already held it at waist level, the gleaming chrome muzzle aimed at Oswald's middle. "Surprised to see me?"

Oswald scowled. His grip on the rifle didn't falter. "You're not supposed to be here."

"Frustrating, isn't it? When things don't go as planned?"

A twitch of a grin snagged the corner of Oswald's mouth. The chameleon hadn't quite mastered every human expression. "How did you find me?"

"That's not important. What matters right now is that you tell me who you're working for. Then we can each be on our way."

Oswald's eyes narrowed like a reptile. "You're not going to stop me?" Then he blinked as if realizing— "Who took your place in the motorcade?"

"Boggles the mind, doesn't it? Who's to say I'm not there right now, and what you're seeing before you is a Jack Kennedy from an entirely different reality?"

"You've been listening to too many of the Greys' stories."

"An *infinite universe with infinite possibilities*—or something like that. They certainly have a way with words."

"They're a slave race. You had your own variety on this planet a century ago. The black-skinned humans. I'm sure they told plenty of their own stories to avoid the horrors of their reality."

Jack raised the incinerator, keeping the muzzle trained on Oswald's head. "Who sent you? The Klaggsrons?" He knew better, but he had to keep the chameleon talking. Sooner or later, the truth would spill out.

"Those brutes know only war. They will decimate your planet. We, on the other hand, have other uses for it."

"How does killing me fit into your grand scheme?"

"*Humans First*, Mr. President. You have already surrendered your nation to alien interests. The Greys walk your streets, taking jobs from honest Americans, and while you speak of how their technology will enrich American lives, what have they done for your people thus far? They are parasites, bottom-feeders. They make great promises, but they will never deliver on them." The chameleon winked awkwardly. "Or so the rhetoric goes."

"You haven't answered my question."

"I forget how obtuse your species can be. *Humans First*. We have ties to every major power in your country: the Democrats, the Republicans, the mob, the CIA, the FBI. Lee Harvey Oswald will not be a *human* assassin." Suddenly, the Chameleon transformed before Jack's eyes into a Grey with a pumpkin-sized head, knotted muscles beneath his dolphin-like skin and long, four-knuckled fingers. "But he will be disguised as a human, of course. The American people will panic. How many of their friends, their enemies, people they pass on the street, are actually *Greys* in similar camouflage?"

Jack's grip on the incinerator tightened as he stared into the abysmal black of the chameleon's expressionless eyes. "It's a lie. The Greys have no such form-changing ability."

"Do you know them so well? Are you sure they have told you everything? Exposed all of their secrets?" Shark teeth flashed in a hideous grin. "Come now, Mr. President, how can you possibly be so naïve? To think—"

The chameleon went up in a cloud of smoke, much like the Klaggsron had in the Oval Office. The rifle clattered to the floor as Jack pocketed the incinerator pistol and made for the window. The motorcade would arrive in moments.

One problem: there was no longer an assassin waiting. Jack cursed his itchy trigger finger and waved away the chameleon's smoke. There was only one thing to be done.

He picked up the rifle and brought the stock to his shoulder, sighting the shot. LB's JFK clone would be seated on Jackie's right in the convertible's backseat, turning to smile and wave at the crowds. The shot would take off the back of the clone's head. Jackie would scramble after it with no idea the man beside her wasn't really her husband at all.

Jack paused as three motorcycle cops came into view, flanking the Lincoln. The crowds on the street below clamored with excitement: whites, blacks, and Greys. Their hero was on his way. They were about to see him in the flesh.

Jack's index finger curled around the trigger.

But he paused. Something wasn't right. He could feel it in his gut.

Maybe it wasn't the time for him to leave Earth. Not now. Not after hearing Oswald's melodramatic soliloquy. With this new chameleon threat, if it turned out to be more than talk, America needed her king more than ever before—alive, and in the White House.

They had six months before the Klaggsrons arrived. The Soviets and Greys could handle the Dark Side stations and Earth Shield for now. Jack had work to do here: root out the form-changers, work with the Greys to find some way to identify them, take down the Humans First organization which, irony aside, had apparently been overrun by these aliens. If Oswald was right, they'd already crept into major positions of power. Jack had to wonder about Hoover at the FBI. Or McCone at the CIA. Hell, maybe even Hoffa. Their enemy was an unseen threat that could change its form, wear anyone's face.

Jack had to get his house in order, as Commandant Perchik had advised.

With a heavy sigh, the President lowered the assassin's rifle as the motorcade passed incredible fanfare below. The JFK clone and Mrs. Kennedy continued en route to the Dallas Trade Mart, unimpeded.

Someone cleared his throat at the door. Jack whirled to face him with the rifle in hand.

"Change of plans?" LB inclined his head to one side, appraising the President with a decidedly Southern wink.

Jack dropped the weapon to his side. "He wasn't acting alone."

LB nodded as if all was in a day's work. "We'll switch out the clone at the luncheon when you take a bathroom break." He cleared his throat—an unnecessary tick for any machine. "Looks like you won't be leaving us so soon."

"Looks that way." Jack fingered the rifle. "Why aren't you with the parade?"

The cyborg shrugged. "Figured something went wrong when I didn't hear any shots. Your Hollywood *oracle* got it wrong, Jack."

Jack shook his head as he met LB at the door. "She saw just one possible future. It's up to us to make a better one."

"You honestly think we can?"

"I don't see anyone else volunteering." He handed the rifle over to LB. "Take care of this, won't you? I have a luncheon to attend."

"This Nation was founded by men of many nations and backgrounds. It was founded on the principle that all men are created equal, and that the rights of every man are diminished when the rights of one man are threatened. Today, we are committed to a worldwide struggle to promote and protect the rights of all who wish to be free. We face, therefore, a moral crisis as a country and a people. It cannot be quieted by token moves or talk. It is a time to act in the Congress, in your State and local legislative body and, above all, in all of our daily lives. It is not enough to pin the blame on others or deplore the facts that we face. A great change is at hand, and our task, our obligation, is to make that revolution, that change, peaceful and constructive for all. Those who do nothing are inviting shame, as well as violence. Those who act boldly are recognizing right, as well as reality."

Jack paused to survey the expectant faces in the audience before him. Jackie smiled warmly up at him. His angel. He nodded to her and continued, his voice filling the silence: "Next week I shall ask the Congress of the United States to act, to make a commitment it has not fully made in this century to the proposition that race has no place in American life or law. This is one country. It has become one country because all of us and all the people who came here had an equal chance to develop their talents. We cannot say to five percent of the population that you can't have that right. They have come to us from a distant star in search of peace. They have not demanded our friendship, only sought our help, and yet many among us have gone out of their way to make them feel unwelcome. I think we owe them and we owe ourselves a better country than that. This is what we're talking about. This is a matter which concerns this country and what it stands for, and in meeting it I ask the support of all our citizens. Thank you very much."

Jack nodded to Governor Connally as he stepped back from the podium, as the Grand Courtyard in the Dallas Trade Mart erupted in thunderous applause, as 2,600 city leaders rose from their tables and half-eaten lunches to show their support for the man who would lead their country into a future brighter than any they could ever imagine.

Or die trying.

> *"The cost of freedom is always high, but Americans have always paid it. And one path we shall never choose, and that is the path of surrender, or submission."*
> – John F. Kennedy

THE
KENNEDY TOUR

by R.H. Blackburn

...and BAM! They were on the streets of Dallas, on that fateful day on November 22, 1963. Phil Hendrix looked down at his period-piece Timex watch on his right wrist and marveled at how warm it was for this time of year. Of course, he thought, we are in Texas in the 1960's after all, but he was always amazed at the weather every time he came back to this scene.

He had the tour group spread out amongst the crowd of native on-lookers gathered around Dealy Plaza at the corners of Main and Houston. All his people were decked out in their 60's dress so as not to disturb the yokels. They were still having fun with it, taking pictures of each other with reproductions of ancient cameras, laughing at their reflections in the quaint storefront glass, and trying to talk as if they belonged in this time period.

Phil smiled. As long as they all didn't freak when it happened, everything would be okay. Most of his customers had done tours like this before, so there shouldn't be any reason for concern, but there were a couple of participants that he felt deserved some special attention. One of the women on the tour had seemed a bit squeamish during his brief introduction before they began and had reacted strongly to his graphic depiction of the assassination. She might be trouble, he thought. Then there was that young man with the Foster Grants and the porkpie hat. He had listened to Phil's run-down on what they would see on the tour and hadn't reacted at all.

A cool customer, Phil thought. He looked at his watch, 12:15. The sun was reflected off the windows of the Texas School Book

Depository across the way, making it difficult to see Oswald as he crouched behind the soot-covered window ledge. In seventeen minutes, this part would be over and they would move on to Oswald being shot by Jack Ruby on his way to County Jail. After that, they would watch a young John F. Kennedy Jr. salute his father's casket at Arlington Cemetery and then the tour was over.

Phil leaned back against the brick facade of the nearby building and watched the proceedings with bored diligence. He saw Orville Nix not far away lift up his Keystone camera and check the viewfinder. Mary Muchmore must be around here somewhere, he thought. They would both shoot film that would almost rival Zapruder's own amateur work in documenting the assassination.

Then he saw Mr. Porkpie Hat step to the curb and glance down at his own Keystone held tightly in his arms as he checked the range and adjusted the lens. He had taken off his glasses, and Phil recognized him right away.

"You're one of them," Phil said sliding up next to Porkpie, not asking, just stating a fact. "You're not thinking about trying anything are you?" He waited until Porkpie took off his hat and tossed it to the curb. "It won't work—they won't even know we're here."

Without the hat, the features were even more pronounced, etching all too familiar lines across the face, the hair, and the piercing blue eyes. On his forehead to one side was the Kennedy Crest, the armored hand holding four arrows between two olive branches, tattooed in royal blue, red and green. He gave Phil Hendrix a look that was both imperious and scornful.

"I know the rules, Mr. Hendrix," he said through gritted teeth. "I'm Miles Kennedy, and I am here not for the first time."

Phil Hendrix gave him a puzzled look. "Why torture yourself? It's done! Been done for two hundred years almost."

Miles Kennedy refused to look at Hendrix. "I've been here seventy-two times, as your records have no doubt told you by now, and each time I come here, I look for the changes." He turned suddenly and Phil Hendrix could see the madness in his eyes. "Every time I come here to this terrible tragedy, it's supposed to be the same, and every time I can pick out something different, something changed." He stopped and took a deep breath and resumed staring at the unraveling nightmare in front of him. "Sometimes it's a bird sitting in the wrong place, or a shadow where there was none before, or something so minute not even *They* notice it, but I do."

Phil Hendrix took a step back and stared hard at Miles Kennedy. He was about to have him pulled from the tour, but his internal network verified to his satisfaction that Kennedy had said this before and never done anything to warrant removal.

"You know what they say," Miles Kennedy continued. "They say there is a curse on this family, a curse that has followed us for more than two hundred years. They say that, but they are wrong."

Suddenly Phil Hendrix just wanted the tour to be over and his shift done for the day.

A silence settled in and Phil hoped that was all he would need to hear, but Kennedy wasn't done. He had only stopped because the open-top black limousine had finally appeared rounding the corner from Houston Street and turning on to Elm Street. As the car rolled past the Book Depository, Miles Kennedy continued.

"There never was a curse," he hissed through clenched teeth. "Someone behind the scenes, behind the curtain, is controlling all this." He brought his camera up and looked through the viewfinder. "I have to use this antiquated junk, but you'll see. Maybe not today, but someday, I will expose this treachery. There is no curse."

Hendrix watched the car, mesmerized, as it slid along the roadway, everyone inside waving. The young President sitting next to his beautiful wife, smiling to the crowd.

"Have you ever considered," Phil Hendrix said to Miles Kennedy as he raised the camera for the telling shot, "that you being here every time is in itself part of the curse?"

A shadow passed across Miles Kennedy's face, and he turned to look Phil Hendrix in the eye.

Hendrix was staring over Kennedy's head as Governor John Connally and his wife, Nellie, came in to view.

"What do you mean by that?" Miles Kennedy had a look of anguish and surprise.

"I mean, you could be the cause of all this," Phil Hendrix said. "It's because you're here that all this happens. It's part of the curse."

Miles Kennedy's face turned red and he started to stammer a

rebuke.

Then it happened, and though it was only lasted seconds, for Hendrix it played out in slow motion, starting with the first shots, then the blood, and finally the screams. People were yelling, shouting, and crying all around him. He hesitated a moment, letting the magnitude of the event sink in, then he went around gathering up his group for departure.

When he had everyone together, he looked to the curb and saw Miles Kennedy kneel down and pick up his hat. He had already put the glasses back on, not wanting to be recognized by the rest of the group. His head was downcast and the camera hung unused in his hand as he joined the group.

Hendrix appraised him and felt a sudden jolt of sorrow for the young man and what he had said to him. He hadn't really been thinking about it—the words just came tumbling out, but the effect they had was unmistakable.

"You gonna be okay?" Phil Hendrix asked the now quiet tour participant.

Miles Kennedy nodded his head in affirmation. "Yeah," he said, "till it gets me, too."

Hendrix looked for a grin but found only a hollow smile and haunted eyes staring at nothing and seeing the same.

AUTHOR BIOGRAPHIES

Nick Andreychuk (*Accidents Happen*) is a Derringer Award-winning mystery writer. His stories have appeared in numerous magazines and anthologies, such as *Austin Layman's Crimestalker Casebook*, *Over My Dead Body!*, *Plan B*, *Sherlock Holmes Mystery Magazine*, *Suspense Magazine*, *Techno Noir*, and *Who Died in Here?*

R.H. Blackburn (*The Kennedy Tour*) makes his first professional sale with this publication.

Patricia Bruce (*Marilyn's Vows*) is a free-lance writer from Western Canada who winters in Arizona. Patricia journals the angst and issues of society through the eyes of a Senior—and with understandings that we can't take life too seriously! You can read Patricia's work in: *Poetry Quarterly*, *Wilderness House Literary Review*, *Mindful Word*, *Calliope*, *Crack the Spine*, *Rusty Nail*, *Eskimo Pie*, *Mouse Tales*, and others.

Gary Cahill (*Fathers, Sons, Ghosts, Guns*) is an Active Member of Mystery Writers of America New York, International Thriller Writers, and Irish American Writers and Artists. His first short story, "That Kind of Guy", was published under the honorary Black Mask banner in the January 2009 *Ellery Queen's Mystery Magazine* and was reprinted in a *Pulp Empire* anthology. "Corner Of River And Rain" was released in online, Kindle, and print anthology formats with *Short Story Me Genre Fiction*, and "The Damnedest Things" ran in *The First Line Literary Journal Fall 2012* (print, PDF, audio, and Kindle). "The Way To A Man's Heart" inaugurated the new online e-mag and e-book anthology from *Plan B Magazine* (Volume 1), and "Ninety Miles, A Million Miles" appears in Volume II. *Shotgun Honey* will feature the flash fiction "Hudson County, November '80" online in Fall 2013. He worked (and still plays) for over 23 years in NYC's Hell's Kitchen, and can now be found across the Hudson River as a staff member at the Weehawken NJ Public Library.

Harri B. Cradoc (*Bobby's Close Shave*) has written fiction and essays for over thirty years. He studied forensics in a U.S. Air Force program designed to train computer science instructors. After many years as a systems administrator, he now teaches computer programming and has developed his own course in cyber security. His home is in Port Dickinson, New York.

Jarrid Deaton *(Out of Frame)* lives and writes in eastern Kentucky. He received his MFA in Creative Writing from Spalding University. His work has appeared in *Underground Voices*, *Thieves Jargon*, *decomP*, *Pear Noir!*, *Big Pulp*, and elsewhere.

A six-time Pushcart nominee, **Liz Dolan** *(Holy Day)* has won an established artist fellowship from the Delaware Division of the Arts. Her second poetry manuscript, *A Secret of Long Life*, which is seeking a publisher, was nominated for the Robert McGovern Prize. Her first poetry collection, *They Abide*, was published by March Street Press.

Milo James Fowler *(The Cost of Freedom)* is a teacher by day and a speculative fictioneer by night. His work has appeared in *AE Science Fiction*, *Cosmos*, and *Shimmer*, and many of his stories are now available on Amazon for Kindle readers. When he's not grading papers, he's imagining what the world might be like in a few dozen alternate realities. www.milojamesfowler.com.

Raymond Gallucci *(How the Mighty Have Fallen)* is a professional engineer who has been writing poetry since 1990. He is an incorrigible rhymer, tending toward the skeptical/cynical regarding daily life. He has been fortunate to have been published in poetry magazines and on-line journals such as *Nuthouse*, *Mother Earth International*, *Feelings/Poets' Paper*, *Möbius*, *Pablo Lennis*, *Muse of Fire*, *So Young!*, *the Aardvark Adventurer*, *Poetic Licencse*, *Thumbprints*, *Unlikely Stories*, *Bibliophilos*, *Fullosia Press*, *Nomad's Choir*, *Hidden Oak*, *Poetsespresso*, *Soul Fountain*, and *Dana Literary Society*.

A.A. Garrison *(Non Compos Mentis)* is a thirty-year-old man living in the mountains of North Carolina. His short fiction has appeared in dozens of zines, anthologies, and web journals, as well as the Pseudopod webcast. He is the author of a post-apocalyptic horror novel, *The End of Jack Cruz*, (Montag Press). He blogs at synchroshock.blogspot.com.

Walter Giersbach's *(No More War Redux)* fiction has appeared in

Bewildering Stories, Every Day Fiction, Everyday Weirdness, Gumshoe Review, Lunch Hour Stories, Mouth Full of Bullets, Mystery Authors, Northwoods Journal, OG Short Fiction, Over My Dead Body, Paradigm Journal, Pif Magazine, Pulp Modern, r.kv.r.y, Short Fiction World, Southern Fried Weirdness, The Short Humour Site, The World of Myth and, of course, *Big Pulp.* Two volumes of short stories, *Cruising the Green of Second Avenue,* published by Wild Child (www.wildchildpublishing.com) are available at Barnes & Noble and other online retailers. He served for three decades as director of communications for Fortune 500 companies, helped publicize the Connecticut Film Festival, managed publicity and programs for Western Connecticut State University's Haas Library, and now moderates a writing group in New Jersey.

John Grey (*Camelot, Mariner Year 1962*) is an Australian-born writer and musician, currently a resident of Providence, RI. He has been published in numerous magazines including *Weird Tales, Christian Science Monitor, Agni, Poet Lore* and *Journal Of The American Medical Association* as well as the horror anthology *What Fears Become,* with work upcoming in *Sanskrit, GW Review* and the *Potomac Review.* He also has had plays produced in Los Angeles and off-off Broadway in New York. John was the winner of a Rhysling Award for short genre poetry in 1999.

Atar Hadari (*The Night Kennedy Got Shot*) was born in Israel, raised in England, and studied poetry in the US. His *Songs from Bialik: Selected Poems of H. N. Bialik* (Syracuse University Press) was a finalist for the American Literary Translators' Association Award, his debut collection, *Rembrandt's Bible* is out now from Indigo Dreams in 2013 and his *Lives of the Dead: Poems of Hanoch Levin* is forthcoming from Arc Publications in 2014.

John Hayes (*Canvassing the Vote, Cuckold, The Plutocrat*) has been published in numerous venues, including *Hungur, Space and Time, Flesh and Blood, Aoife's Kiss, Thema, BareBone, Modern Haiku, Tales of the Talisman, Writers Journal, Premonitions, NFG,* and *Big Pulp.* He sculpts, acts and directs in community theater, and once appeared as a scurvy-looking corpse on Homicide. Seven of his one-act plays have been produced.

L.L. Hill (*KC*) is currently resident again in northern Canada, where she continues to read, write and practice photography.

Jack Horne (*Two Brothers Fighting, A Lonely Actress, A Patsy?*) lives in

Plymouth, England, where he works for the local theatre. A number of his poems, short stories and articles have been published and also a collection of plays.

Tony Laplume (*The Cuban Exile Crisis*) graduated from the University of Maine in 2003. While there he worked on the *Maine Campus* newspaper and helped found the student literary journal *Hemlock*. He has since published a variety of material, including the superhero novel *The Cloak of Shrouded Men*, the short story collection *Monorama*, the poetry volume *Terror of Knowing*, and the comic book biography of Mikhail Prokhorov from Bluewater Press. He edited the microfiction collection entitled *Mouldwarp Press Presents #1 "Project Mayhem,"* and his work has appeared in the anthologies *Villainy* and *The Temporal Element*. His most recent published work is *Yoshimi Trilogy Vol. 1: Yoshimi and the Shadow Clan*.

Tim Lieder (*Mountain Of God*) has been published in *Silverthought, Everyday Fiction, Shock Totem,* and *Big Pulp*. Additionally, Tim owns and operates Dybbuk Press through which he's edited and published eight titles including *God Laughs When You Die* by Michael Boatman and *Teddy Bear Cannibal Massacre*. His latest title is a multi-author horror anthology based on the Bible entitled *She Nailed a Stake Through His Head*. Another Bible-themed anthology, *King David and the Spiders from Mars*, is scheduled for publication in 2014.

Paul Lorello (*Last Will of Little Rosie*) is a freelance writer from Ronkonkoma, New York. He recently finished his first novel and will one day write a second. His vitamin D is low. He likes science fiction and cats. He knows very little about everything.

Zoe McAuley (*Debts of the Father*) grew up near Belfast, but now lives in the grim north of England. She spent several years at Durham University learning to stare at old walls in great detail. She has been searching for gainful employment, but in its absence, she has taken to writing short stories and performing in an improvised comedy troupe. This is her third published story—she's keeping count at zoe-mcauley.tumblr.com.

Terrence McCauley (*A Bullet's All it Takes*) is an award-winning writer of crime fiction. His latest novel, *Slow Burn,* is available from Noir Nation Books. His first book, *Prohibition*, published by Airship 27, is a full-length novel set in the colorful, exciting world of 1930

New York City. A prequel to this novel, *Fight Card: Against the Ropes*, was published by Fight Card Books in 2013. A proud native of The Bronx, NY, he is currently working on his next work of fiction. E-mail Terrence at terrencepmccauley@gmail.com.

A native New Yorker, **James Penha** (*Camelot*) has lived for the past twenty years in Indonesia. He has been nominated for Pushcart Prizes in fiction and in poetry. *Snakes and Angels*, a collection of his adaptations of classic Indonesian folk tales, won the 2009 Cervena Barva Press fiction chapbook contest; *No Bones to Carry*, a volume of his poetry, the 2007 New Sins Press Editors' Choice Award. His earlier chapbooks of poetry were *Greatest Hits* (Pudding House: 2011) and *On the Back of the Dragon* (Omega Cat Press: 1992). Waterways selected lines from his many contributions to that litmag as its 2011-2012 themes for submissions. Penha edits *The New Verse News*, an online journal of current-events poetry.

Terrie Leigh Relf (*The Curse of Brian Boru*) is on staff at Alban Lake Publishing where she edits *Blood Bond*, *Disturbed Digest*, and *Illumen*, and hosts The Drabble contest. She is a lifetime member of The Science Fiction Poetry Association, an active member of the Horror Writers Association, and a lover of conspiracy theories. Recent releases include *The Waters of Nyr*, *The Poet's Workshop—and Beyond*, and *The Ancient One, Book II of the Blood Journey Saga*, co-authored with Henry Lewis Sanders. They are currently at work on *Book III, Children of Blood*.

James Frederick William Rowe (*Rosemary's Lobotomy, Salute, Goin' to the Moon*) is a young poet and author out of Brooklyn, New York, with works appearing in *Heroic Fantasy Quarterly*, *Andromeda Spaceways*, *Tales of the Talisman*, *Bete Noire*, and most notably, *Big Pulp*. When not writing fantasy, science fiction, and horror fiction and poetry, he is pursuing a Ph.D. in philosophy, is an adjunct professor, and works in a variety of freelance positions. Unlike the poems to appear in *Apeshit*, the author's late grandmother Elizabeth Sundberg (1918-2011) would not object to those presented here. James' website can be reached at http://jamesfwrowe.wordpress.com.

E.F. Schraeder (*The Winners*) is a member of the New England Horror Writers who reads, writes, and loves all things weird and quiet. Her creative work has recently appeared or is forthcoming in *Carnival of the Damned, Flashes in the Dark, Dark Gothic Magazine Res-*

urrected, *Zombie Jesus and Other True Stories*, and elsewhere. Her poetry chapbook, *The Hunger Tree*, is available from Finishing Line Press. She studied literature and philosophy in grad school and probably wears too much paisley.

Mike Sharlow (*Body Dump*) lives in a small city in the Midwest along the banks of the Mississippi River. He has published numerous short stories and three novels. His website is www.mikesharlowwriter.com.

R.J. Spears (*Boiler Room Girl*) lives in Columbus, Ohio and writes mystery/crime and horror fiction. His stories have appeared across the web at *Shotgun Honey*, *Out of the Gutter*, the *Horror Zine*, and *Flashes in the Dark*, along with several other sites. His novella, "Forget the Alamo", reached #55 on Amazon's Free Bestseller List for Horror. His novel, *Sanctuary from the Dead*, was just released by J. Ellington Ashton Press. You can learn more about his writing at rjspears.com.

Anna Sykora (*Hannah's Darling*) has been an attorney in New York and teacher of English in Germany, where she resides with her patient husband and three enormous cats. To date she has placed 124 tales, mostly genre, in the small press, and almost three hundred poems. Motto: eat your rejections like pretzels.

Sarah Delap U (*Ode to O's Clothes*) is a writer and musician currently living in Brooklyn, N.Y. She works with ebooks by day, and is a member of superhero rock band **The Super Friends** by night, where she plays saxophone as Hawk Girl. Her articles have been published in the *Barnes and Noble Review*, *New York Daily News*, *Country Living Magazine*, and *Time Out Istanbul in English*. Her poetry has appeared in the *Apeiron Review*, *Wrong Brain*, and *The Opium Jar*. A Former Trekkie, she is absolutely terrified of outer space.

Gay warlocks, lesbian warriors, transgender femmes fatale, bi-curious neighbors, dyke drug addicts, super-queerees, fag freedom fighters, boys in uniform, doctors, astronauts, murderers, prison bitches, drag queens &

Clones, Fairies & Monsters in the Closet

Order online at exterpress.com/catalog/monstersinthecloset

BIG PULP

summer 2013 $12.00

"Catskin"
by
Arley Sorg

...and other stories

The son of a smalltown sheriff takes crime prevention into his own hands, but curiosity may kill the cat in Arley Sorg's "Catskin," (illustration by Phil Good). This issue features 20+ more horror, SF, fantasy, mystery, & romance stories & poems!

For contents and ordering details, visit:
exterpress.com/bigpulp/summer2013

BIG PULP

spring 2013 $12.00

"A Question of Storage"

by John Bowker

A massive collection of pornography inspires a brilliant student to explore the limits of the human mind in John Bowker's "A Question of Storage." This issue features 25 horror, SF, fantasy, & mystery stories and poems!

For contents and ordering details, visit:
exterpress.com/bigpulp/spring2013